OVERWATCH®

D0032396

THE HERO OF NUMBANI

OVERWATCH®

THE HERO OF NUMBANI

by

Nicky Drayden

Scholastic Inc.

©2020 Blizzard Entertainment, Inc. All rights reserved. Overwatch and Blizzard Entertainment are trademarks or registered trademarks of Blizzard Entertainment, Inc., in the U.S. and/or other countries.

ISBN 978-1-338-57597-2

10 9 8 7 6 5 4 3 2 1   20 21 22 23 24

Printed in the U.S.A.   23

First printing 2020
Book design by Betsy Peterschmidt
Cover illustration by Odera Igbokwe

CHAPTER 1

Warm, golden light filtered in through the window in Efi's workshop, bringing with it a beam of hope . . . Hope that this new robot of hers would work this time, and not embarrass her in front of her friends. Again.

Efi watched as the six-legged spider ran across the wooden tabletop. It was made of jet-black metal and the most advanced artificial intelligence Efi's ingenuity and allowance could afford. She held her breath as it approached the edge. This robot would revolutionize the world, Efi was sure of it, but right now it had one big problem.

Thump.

The robot toppled over the table's edge and hit the ground. Then, as if dazed, it stumbled around, wobbling this way and that. Finally, it seemed as if it had corrected its footing, and took a few confident steps . . . right into the side of the unlaced sneaker belonging to Efi's best friend Naade.

Naade frowned and picked up the robot, its legs waving in

the air like an agitated crab. "Not too smart, is it?" he asked.

"Not yet," Efi said, carefully taking the robot back from her friend. "But it's going to be. Everyone's going to want one of these."

The spatial processing freeware she'd downloaded had serious bugs in it. Nothing she couldn't fix, of course, but that'd take time, and she already had 150 customers waiting on their orders. From the corner of her workshop, the "new sale" alert on her laptop chirped. Efi flinched.

Make that 151 customers . . .

Don't get her wrong—Efi was truly grateful for all the interest her robot prototype had stirred up on Hollagram: 1,023 likes and 850 claps and 332 shares. But somewhere between taking the first order and making the first production unit, she realized that she'd gotten in way over her head. As always, Efi had big dreams and not enough hands to make those dreams real. She was hoping Naade and Hassana—her best friends since that unfortunate science fair incident a few years back—would volunteer once they saw how revolutionary the robot would be, but her demonstration wasn't going very well.

"I want one already," said Hassana, a sharp grin on her face. "I can't even contain my excitement for owning a six-legged robot that's awesome at falling off tables."

"Ha, funny," Efi said, setting the robot on the workbench again and herding it away from the edges with her cupped hands. Maybe the robot was clumsy, but she was sure her friends would be impressed by what she had to show them next. Efi pressed a silver button on the bug's back, and a life-sized, holographic projection of Naade flickered into view, sitting cross-legged on the table. It blinked at the real Naade.

"Whoa!" Naade said, examining the hologram from all angles—from the mismatched socks peeking under the pants of his school uniform, to the stewed-beans stain on the lapel of his shirt, to the scar on his forehead from the battle he'd lost to the NO PARKING sign in front of Kọfi Aromo. "You're right. Everyone's gonna want one of these."

"Never mind. You can count me out," said Hassana. "One Naade in my life is plenty. Though if swapping this one for the other is possible . . ."

Naade stuck his tongue out at Hassana, but Hassana pretended not to notice and instead swiped her hand across the projection, dragging her fingers through it like it was holographic finger paint. The image dissipated where she touched it, and then the pixels reassembled. The Naade hologram turned its head toward her and smiled. Hassana shivered.

"No one's swapping anyone for anything," Efi said to her best friends. "And I'm not building an army of Naades, if that's what you're thinking. It's called a Junie, short for 'Junior Assistant,' designed to serve as a stand-in for social and professional situations. Like if you are unable to make a meeting, you can send your Junie to take video and report back with a transcript of the events."

"You mean I could fall asleep during history class, and it'd take notes for me?" Naade asked, his eyes wide.

Efi frowned. It could do that, in fact, but Naade sounded a little too enthusiastic about the idea. "This isn't your excuse to goof off in class," Efi said, shaking her head. "Naade-Junior, please tell my friend here why it's important that he take his studies seriously."

The holoimage nodded, flickering as it retrieved audio from a voice test that Efi had recorded earlier. Finally, the holoimage opened its mouth to speak, but out came a dizzying mix of English, Yoruba, Pidgin, French, and maybe Cantonese, its arms flailing all over the place as it spoke.

"Stop it, Naade!" Efi commanded, exasperated, but once she got her wits back, she remembered she was talking to an AI and not her friend. "Naade-Junior, halt processing!"

The Junie quietly composed itself, then flickered out, leaving nothing but a trail of dust motes stirring in the air.

"Yeah, I definitely consider that an improvement on Naade's usual noise," Hassana said, laughing into her fist.

But Naade noticed how upset Efi was and draped an arm over her shoulder. "I don't know a lot about programming robots or AI, but I do know that nobody gets it right on the first try," he said softly.

"I know." Efi sniffed. She'd started making robots when most kids her age were still stacking alphabet blocks. Bugs were perfectly normal. She usually expected one or two. What she didn't expect was a complete and total disaster. "It's just, I've got all these orders already, and everyone's so excited to get their

Junie. I've been spending all my extra time in the workshop, try-ing to get this thing perfected."

"Well, what can we help with?" asked Hassana, pulling a metal stool up to the worktable. "You know we've got your back."

Efi perked up. She knew they had her back. You don't go through three hours of being stuck to the floor of the school library due to a dysfunctional graviton beam and not come out friends for life. "Okay. If you could work on assembling the legs to the chassis, that would be great." Efi pointed to two boxes on the worktable, brimming with robot parts. "It'll take a little sol-dering and some circuitry work, but I've got this to help."

Efi turned on the huge holographic monitor hanging on her wall and cued up a video.

"Oh! A movie? Is it starring Kam Kalu?" asked Naade, attempt-ing to mimic the macho, one-raised-brow smolder of one of his favorite Nollywood action heroes. And failing. Miserably.

"Actually, it's more like an instructional video on cable colors and terminals, and the most efficient way to calibrate—" Efi gave her friends a bashful smile. "It's probably just easier to watch the video. You're sure you don't mind helping?"

"Isn't making robots how everyone spends their Friday night?" Naade said, holding up a pair of pigtailed wire connections under his nose like a handlebar mustache.

"Yeah, and how hard could it be?" Hassana said, aiming a sol-der gun at a pile of servo motors and making pew, pew noises.

"Ummm . . ." Efi said, wincing. "You're holding that the wrong way." She turned the solder gun around and flicked the switch, and a pale blue light beamed out from it.

Naade laughed so hard, he nearly fell off his stool. "You almost soldered your eyebrows together," he said to Hassana. "Ha, just imagine me walking into school on Monday and telling everyone that you'd pulled an Isaac!"

"So I made a mistake," Hassana said. "But how could you compare me to Isaac?"

"Oh, the way he walked around with his palm stuck to his forehead! Instant classic."

Efi paused the video. "What are you two talking about?" she asked.

"Oh, nothing," Hassana said. "Just a little incident in the science lab today."

"*Little* incident?" Naade said, becoming overly animated with his arms flailing about, just as Naade-Junior had. At least Efi had gotten that part right. "It was only the most stunning, stupendous, ridiculously awesome science lab disaster ev–" Naade sucked in a breath as Hassana elbowed him in the ribs. She gave him a stern look; then he straightened up. "Yeah, it wasn't anything. You didn't miss much."

Efi bit her lip. Left out of her school's best in-jokes yet again. Such was her life. She'd started taking advanced math and science classes her first year of elementary school. Halfway through the academic year, she was placed in junior-high classes. By the end of the next year, she'd taught herself algebra and geometry. Now she was taking courses at the senior high school after lunch, which she mostly loved—International Baccalaureate instruction in calculus and physics—but she missed out on so much of what was going on in school with Naade and Hassana. And lately, that feeling was growing.

"Tell me about it?" Efi begged. "Please?"

"You just had to be there, Efi," Naade said. "Sorry I mentioned it. I'll be more careful next time."

"No, I want to know. It sounds so hilarious!" Efi stretched a smile across her face the best she could. She didn't want her friends to feel sorry for her. She just wanted to be included.

"Okay . . ." Naade said reluctantly. "Well, you know how Isaac is always trying to impress everyone?"

Efi laughed loudly. "Attention seeker, for sure."

Naade raised an eyebrow. "It's more sad than funny. He tries too hard, but he means well. Anyway, Isaac brought a military-grade barrier into science lab during our discussion on semipermeable objects. Where he got such advanced tech, I don't know, but apparently the barrier's instructions were in Omnicode, and Isaac claimed he could read them."

Efi laughed again, certain that this was the hilarious part of the story. A non-augmented *human* reading something as complex as Omnicode? Efi had studied the omnic's written language for nearly three years, and she couldn't understand more than the occasional word here and there. If she couldn't read Omnicode, the chances Isaac could were slim-to-none. Efi's laughter morphed into a forced cough, but Naade gave her another blank stare. She put a pensive look back on her face and nodded. "Okay, go on."

Naade continued. "In any case, Isaac ended up activating the barrier around his head and one of his hands, making it look like they were caught inside a fishbowl. Thankfully, his face was pressed up against the side that let air get through . . ."

Efi bit her lip, reluctant to laugh again. Was this it? Was that the punch line? Had Isaac "pulled an Isaac" yet? She waited so long to respond that Naade shrugged.

"You really had to be there," he finally relented. "Come on. Let's watch this instructional video. I still haven't given up that Kam Kalu is going to be in it. He could act in anything."

"Spoiler alert: He's not. But I can put on a little music in the background while we work. 'We Move Together as One'?" Efi asked, already dancing to the beat of her favorite Lúcio song to shake away the feeling of missing out.

"You know it!" Hassana said, joining in.

Efi and Hassana were in a constant competition to prove who was actually the biggest Lúcio fan. It mainly played out by one-upping each other as they memorized every possible personal detail and fact about their favorite activist/DJ/hero. For example, Efi knew he wore size forty-two skates. She knew his sonic amplifier could hit a target up to eight meters away. She even knew the exact song that Lúcio had played when he led the popular uprising that drove the oppressive Vishkar Corporation out of the first favela—"Rejuvenescência," a song of healing and regrowth. Efi always thought the song was fitting: And though the wounds the corporation left in the community were deep and many, Lúcio knew they would heal, in time.

Hassana's knowledge, on the other hand, seemed to be more trivial in nature . . . like the depth of Lúcio's navel, the type of floss he used, and his favorite food, pão de queijo—little round cheese breads that Hassana liked to prepare on the anniversary of the day she first heard Lúcio's music. Naade was no less a fan, though he made a point to stay out of his friends' heated rivalry.

Naade and Hassana finished watching the instructional video and got to work. They were both quick learners, so Efi had confidence they'd be able to assemble at least two dozen Junies, which gave her the space she needed to work on the bugs in the code. She tucked into her programming interface, a bowl of Lúcio-Oh's cereal at her fingertips, as the steady beat of the music playing helped her fall into a trance. Line by line, she fixed the holes in the logic, then ran the Junie motion simulators on her computer.

The processors revved up in a high-pitched whine that peaked above the music. Efi's computer was overdue for an upgrade, but she couldn't afford to pour more time and money into it right this moment, not when there was so much to do. So she waited patiently as the simulations struggled to compile. It took forever, but finally, little wire-frame versions of the robot skittered across her screen, avoiding obstacles. The simulations succeeded at skirting the table edges. Now it was time to update the Junie's firmware and see if it worked in real life as well.

Efi looked up from her monitor and noticed the room had gotten darker. It was evening already. Only four Junies sat on the workbench, corralled under an overturned crate. Naade sat at his workstation, an upturned robot sitting in a clamp. He was flipping the servos that controlled the hydraulic legs so they kept time with the song playing.

"Naade!" Efi said. "Please try to stay on task. I know it's not the most glamorous way to spend the weekend, but our work is important."

"Sorry, boss," he said, then whispered something to Hassana that Efi couldn't hear, and they both started laughing again.

As they worked, Efi's smile began to hurt, but she plastered it on her face anyway to keep her true feelings tamped down. Yes, Efi, Hassana, and Naade were three best friends, but there was a sort of unspoken feeling that Naade and Hassana were both *Efi's* best friends, while Naade and Hassana seemed to tolerate each other at best. Normally, they teased and poked fun at each other, and at worst, there'd been a couple of bad arguments.

But now, that distance between them was closing, and for every in-joke Efi was left out of, she felt more and more alone. Stuck between worlds. The teenagers in her high school classes had in-jokes of their own, ones that completely flew over her head, ones that she had no earthly chance of decoding.

"Efi?" came her mother's voice from the workshop door. She peeked in and saw Naade and Hassana. "Oh goodness. Hello! I didn't know you all were back here."

"Good evening, Auntie Fola," said Hassana and Naade

together in the same singsong voice, as if they'd rehearsed it a dozen times together.

"Efi put us to work," Naade said, raising up a half-assembled Junie.

"Is that so?" Mother asked. She wore a cheerful, bright blue buba—a loose blouse with flowing sleeves—paired with candy-pink beaded necklaces. Mother loved wearing vibrant colors, and she had the plump cheeks and kind eyes that came from doing years of social work within their community. Efi was proud of that work, but it also meant Mother was constantly trying to help Efi solve problems she didn't necessarily want solved. "Efi, dear. Can I have a word?"

Efi's shoulders slumped. She was about to get *the talk* again, but she followed her mother out into the hall anyway.

"Honey, when I asked you to hang out with your friends more, this isn't what I had in mind."

"They volunteered for it!" Efi said in her own defense.

"I know. They're good friends. But everything in your life can't center around robots. Why don't you take them out to do something fun? Go-kart racing. Or go to the arcade and play some video games. Or mini golf!"

"Mini golf, Mama?"

"Well, I don't know what you kids do for fun these days!"

Then Efi felt even worse. She didn't really know, either. She spent all her time in her workshop or studying or at school. She hated to admit it, but there wasn't a whole lot of time for fun . . . at least not in the traditional sense. To Efi, *work* was fun.

She loved inventing, although to most people—including her mother—it looked like she was working herself to the bone.

Another round of laughter came from Efi's workshop, and the frown on her face deepened.

"What's wrong, dear?" Mother asked. "You look troubled."

Efi sighed. "It's Naade and Hassana."

"Have they been fighting again?"

"No. It's *worse*. They've been getting along."

"That's good, isn't it? Normally, they're bickering like jackals."

Efi shrugged. "I guess I just wish we could go back to the way it was. When we were all in the same classes."

"Relationships can get complicated, but all that means is you're growing up. Maturing . . ." Mother drew out the word "maturing" like she was at a dinner party drinking fancy teas. Like this was a little joke, and not Efi's social life crumbling to bits.

Efi knew she couldn't go back to basic math classes, but maybe she could help her friends catch up to her level. She could build them both a robotic tutor, customized to teach them during their every waking hour. Or maybe she could talk them into getting cybernetic brain upgrades—just like Sojourn, one of Efi's favorite heroes from the old *Overwatch* cartoons, based on Overwatch's real-life former captain.

"Never mind, Mama. I'll figure it out myself," Efi said.

"I know you will. But remember, this isn't something you can logic your way out of. Naade and Hassana are real people with real emotions and real needs."

"Yes, Mama," Efi said, but as she crept back into her work-shop, seeing all those Junie parts piled on the table gave her an idea, one that would let her keep in touch with her friends all day long without having to inject bionic neurons into anyone's brain.

Her mother huffed, probably sensing that Efi was caught up in her own thoughts again. "And, contrary to popular belief, you can't solve *all* your problems with robots."

"Yes, Mama," Efi said again out loud, but thought to herself: *Watch me*.

When Efi rejoined her friends in the workshop, she was giddy with excitement. She took a deep breath, inhaling all the posi-tive energy lingering in the air of her favorite place. This space had been her playroom when she was a toddler, once covered in primary colors and plushy cartoon monsters with big, friendly eyes, but slowly she had dissected her toys, turning her talking dolls and light-up electronics into piles of circuitry and actuators and sensors. And once she'd figured out how they worked, she started building creations of her own. Efi's parents hadn't been too happy at first, seeing all those expensive toys meet their untimely demise, but one day, they brought home a robotics kit for their inquisitive daughter, and the rest was history.

"All right," Efi said to her friends. "Let's try this again." Her optimism was infectious, and soon they were all gathered around the workshop table, cheering on the little Junie as it nav-igated toward the edge, centimeter by centimeter, and just when there wasn't any space left, it stopped, turned, and moved along the perimeter. It was a small success, but Efi swelled with pride, and once she'd done a little more testing, she uploaded the new firmware to all the bots they'd assembled. Hassana and Naade packaged them up in their boxes, ready for shipping.

"A dozen in one day," Naade said, nodding at the stack of Junie boxes. "That's twelve customers who will soon be very happy."

"Make that ten customers," Efi said.

Hassana looked up suddenly. "What? Did you get some cancellations?"

"No," Efi said, pulling down two boxes from the stack. "But I want you each to have one to take with you to school."

"Sweet!" Naade pumped his fist. "Now all I need to do is hide a little pillow in my backpack and—"

"No sleeping through class, Naade," Efi cut in. "I was thinking the Junies could follow you around, see what you see . . . and report back to me. That way, when I go to my high school classes after lunch, I won't miss anything that's going on."

Hassana's smile turned slowly downward, and Naade shook his head, probably remembering that fateful day in the school library when Efi had asked for two volunteers to help her demonstrate her science fair project. *You accidentally overamplify a gravity field one time, and no one ever lets you forget it*, Efi thought. She'd had dozens of successful inventions since, and no one had gotten hurt.

"Please?" Efi asked. "Just try it out. Think of it as a test run. Maybe it'll help boost sales, too! Come on. What could go wrong?"

HollaGram

Junie Backer Update #4

I've been in the workshop every free moment I can find, and I'm excited to announce that we are shipping the first Junies TODAY!!! Thank you so much for your patience. And your support! I couldn't do this without you!

Check your messages for status updates for when your Junior Assistant will arrive, and don't forget to post holovids of you and your new robot in the comments!

REACTIONS

COMMENTS (23)

BackwardsSalamander Awesome! Can't wait for mine!

RealDealDuckBill I wish I had mine right now!

NaadeForPrez Got mine ALREADY! If you hear someone snoring during history class next week, it isn't me!

Read more ...

CHAPTER 2

Ms. Okorie scribbled furiously on the classroom's holographic monitor, writing a calculus function that peeled away from the screen, letter by number by math operator, then hovered five centimeters in front of the surface. To Efi, she was something like a DJ, the way she worked the front of the classroom, but instead of dropping beats, she was dropping equations. She worked the problem, navigating through coordinates and constants and derivatives, while 3-D tangent models spun next to her like backup dancers. Normally, Efi would bob her head along, solving the equation on her tablet at her desk, but today she just couldn't concentrate.

Efi kept her eye on the LIVE FEED button flashing on her screen. She'd linked up to Hassana's and Naade's Junie robots, but so far she'd resisted looking at the feed, because while Ms. Okorie was a pleasant enough teacher, you definitely didn't want to be on her bad side. Still, the temptation was real, and Efi couldn't stop wondering what her friends were doing this very instant.

Had anyone "pulled an Isaac" in the science lab today?

Maybe she'd just take a *little* peek.

She pressed the button and was met with an image of Naade walking through the hallway, beatboxing to himself. The Junie's cameras offered 360 degrees of visibility, meaning if something *was* happening, Efi wouldn't miss a thing. He hung a left, passing the art classroom, and Efi was able to catch a glimpse inside. In that half an instant, she thought she saw Stevie Igwe passing a note to Sibe Oye.

A *paper* note. Whatever was written on it had to be something so important, so private, that he wouldn't risk it getting caught up in the school's digital filters. And that was scandalous enough, but it was a well-known fact that Stevie and Sibe hated each other. Sibe was the president of the student council, and Stevie was captain of the debate team and a devil's advocate on every issue that could possibly cause offense to someone, somewhere. Stevie had heckled Sibe during her entire campaign, particularly on her ideas about having a special appreciation day for the omnic staff at the school. Stevie hated the idea, claiming that omnics were already a liability and not to be trusted, and that at any moment, their school could break out into a miniature Omnic Crisis.

Efi scrunched her nose up. She didn't care for Stevie much, and thankfully, there weren't many people in Numbani who thought like he did. However, her interest was piqued over the paper note, if that's truly what she'd seen. She paused the image and zoomed in, but it was too blurry to make out the object for sure.

Wait, Hassana had art class right now. Efi switched feeds, wound back thirty seconds, and saw Hassana painting strokes on her canvas. The Junie must have been perched on her shoulder. She was creating a self-portrait, lines crisp and colors deep. Hassana was never one to miss details, and Efi had no doubt that every single braid upon her friend's head was accounted for in her painting, all of them sweeping into a neat knot up top.

Efi swiveled the feed to see the rear of the classroom, catching a blurred image of Naade as he walked past in the hallway. In that exact moment, Efi saw what she thought she'd imagined.

A note passing. And a definite smile shared between the two.

This was big.

This was *huge*.

This was—

A message from Efi's cousin and classmate, Dayo, popped up on her screen:

Teacher's coming.

Efi slid the feed closed, quickly brought the equation back up, and started furiously scribbling at solving it. Ms. Okorie's powerful perfume suddenly overwhelmed Efi, and still looking down, she could see the bottom of her teacher's skirt as she stopped beside Efi's desk.

"Efi," she said. "If you're not too busy, could you please show the class how to solve for the y-coordinate?"

Efi cleared her throat. "Yes, ma." And she stood up, passing Dayo's desk. He looked up, concern on his brow. She mouthed *thank you* to her cousin for sending the message. He nodded and looked back down at his tablet before Ms. Okorie's wrath befell him as well.

Efi stood at the front of the classroom, finger to her temple like she was thinking really hard. She knew how to find the solution. She was actually three chapters ahead in her lessons, but she'd learned quickly that teenagers, even smart teenagers in IB calculus classes, didn't like being shown up by almost twelve-year-olds. It wasn't like she was being dishonest, though . . . She'd never fake like she didn't know an answer, but a little acting went a long way. Finally, she made the "aha!" gesture that meant she'd figured it all out, and began to solve the equation. She dusted her hands when she was done and began to return to her seat, but instead of the "Very good, Efi," she was used to hearing from her teacher, Ms. Okorie said, "Very close, Efi. Can someone show her where she went wrong?"

Efi stood stock-still as her teacher called on Dayo. He grabbed his cane and walked up to the front of the room, then swiped away the bottom fourth of her work. The pixels dissolved out of existence, providing him with a clean slate. He solved the problem, and it became immediately apparent where Efi had made her mistake. How could she have been so sloppy?

She knew how. Instead of keeping her mind on her studies, she'd spent half the class period goofing off. Hadn't she just warned Naade about the same thing? Efi needed to focus on being here instead of worrying over what her friends were up to.

"Wonderful," Ms. Okorie said, right as the bell dismissed the class. "Please do exercises Thirty-Four A, B, and C for tomorrow. Don't forget to clearly show your work!"

Efi packed her satchel and tried to walk quickly out of the room, but her cousin followed close behind. Dayo's school uniform looked almost like formal wear on him. No doubt that he'd tailored it himself, adding gold embellishments to the school's emblem and the stitching around the cuffs—enough to get noticed in the halls, but not so much to draw the attention of teachers and administrators. He wore his hair in the tiniest of twists—one hundred fifty-seven of them, he'd once told Efi, for his favorite prime number. Efi had suffered through the misfortune of asking why it was his favorite prime number. He'd said that numbers held important meanings and then delved into an impromptu math history lesson with more tangents than Ms. Okorie could ever fit on her holoboard.

"Efi, wait up. Where are you running off to?" Dayo asked as he cut Efi off from her speedy exit.

"I don't know. I just need some air. I've never messed up like that before, in front of *everyone*."

"Nobody's perfect all the time."

Efi nodded. She knew she wasn't perfect. She'd once gotten a B on a science project. And then there was that time she'd gotten her hair trapped in the gears of one of her robot's motors. Dayo had been there for that fiasco as well, and thanks to his handy scissor work, he'd salvaged most of her bangs. Now she wore her hair natural, twisted and tied back into a ponytail, out of the way and far from the reach of her experiments.

Yes, she made mistakes, but she learned from them.

"What were you looking at, anyway?" Dayo asked. "You were squinting so hard at your tablet, I thought you were about to fall into it."

"A live feed from the Junies I gave Naade and Hassana. I love being here and learning at your school for part of the day, but I feel like I'm missing out with my friends."

"Hey, this is *your* school, too. And you've definitely got friends here!"

"You? You have to be my friend. We're cousins."

"Nah, if you weren't cool, I'd just as soon pretend you didn't exist." Dayo nudged Efi in the shoulder. "I saw my brother at the tram concourse a few weeks ago, right as the doors were closing. I could have stuck my hand out and held them open, but I just straight ignored him."

"Ooh," Efi said, sucking in her breath. "Did you tell Auntie you saw him?"

"Nah, no reason to get her upset all over again. Anyway, Bisi's chosen his path, and if you ask me, he deserves a lot worse than a tram door closing in his face."

Bisi was Dayo's older brother, but they hadn't talked to him in well over a year now. Efi understood why Dayo was bitter about seeing him, but that didn't erase all the good memories Efi had of hanging out with him. Bisi had even given Efi her first tool set . . . Not like the plastic set her parents had gotten her for her fourth birthday, but real, carbon-steel tools. Bisi was smart. Smarter than Dayo, probably. He could have done something great with his life.

But after high school, he'd gotten caught up with some bad people. He'd owed those bad people some sort of debt, and when they came to collect, they'd mistaken Dayo for Bisi. They'd collected their debt by beating Dayo up, leaving him with a shattered hip, a severe concussion, and a big, shameful stain upon their family.

Bisi had come to see Dayo in the hospital, muttering apologies, and then just . . . disappeared. Sometimes Efi wondered if Dayo would be glad to see his brother come home, once he got over his anger. Just like Efi would.

"Hey, Dayo!" called a guy from down the hallway. "This little lady giving you grief?" He laughed.

"You know my cousin Efi," Dayo said. "Efi, this is Sam."

"Yeah! The brainiac, right?" Sam said, staring at Efi like he was waiting for her to perform a mathemagical trick and pull an irrational number out of her sleeve or something. Efi hated that look, which was almost always accompanied by some variation of "Say something smart."

She wanted to fit in, not stand out.

"Efi's having trouble making friends here," Dayo said, giving Sam a shrug.

Efi's eyes widened. Oh no, he didn't just say that, did he? She felt horrified and beyond embarrassed. "I . . . uh, have to go.

Don't want to miss my tram!" And then Efi got out of there as fast as she could. Efi loved Dayo, she really did. He was nice to her. He even let her call him by just his first name at school, so she'd feel like his peer and not his kid cousin obligated to show respect. But sometimes he could be majorly clueless.

Efi hopped on the #47 tram from school to home. Outside the tram windows, all of Numbani sped past: a sleek, high-tech skyline nestled within swaths of nature and sprawling beauty. The glass on the buildings blended into the too big, too blue sky, and nearly every tiered balcony boasted a garden of some sort, so that it was difficult to tell where the structures ended and nature began. On one terrace she saw omnics and humans working together to tend a terrarium bursting with orchids. Efi could almost feel the energies flowing through her city, like it was *breathing*, uniting its people in harmony. She sometimes heard her mother and aunt speaking of the òrìṣà, spiritual beings who were an integral part of the natural world and touched their lives in ways Efi was still struggling to understand. She'd tried to ask questions on how technology and AI fit into it all, but she was usually swatted away.

Efi sighed as she popped in her earbuds and turned her attention to her tablet. The live feed was just Naade snoring in class, and Hassana was mumbling to herself during a spelling quiz, so Efi switched to archive footage and rewound through the day.

Then she found something. Between fourth and fifth period, Stevie Igwe and Sibe Oye were holding hands!

Efi texted Hassana as soon as school was out.

I can't believe Stevie and Sibe are a thing!

Were a thing. Lasted a whole two hours.

Really?

U should have seen the breakup. Epic.

Wait. Let me find it. What time was it?

Dunno. After gym sometime.

Efi scrolled through the feed to after Hassana's gym class. And there it was. This was it! But everything was dark. Efi could barely make out muffled screaming. And name calling. Sounded like Sibe was saying Stevie was a "backwoods stinking alligator with an ice cream cart"? Or maybe she'd said "backward-thinking omnic-hater with an ice cube for a heart"? It was hard to tell.

What's going on?
I can't see your feed from then.

Ah, oh. I stashed my Junie in my backpack @ gym. Didn't want any of those sticky-fingered basketball girls to fab it. I forgot to take it back out right away.

Sorry.

Efi went to Naade's feed from the same time. Maybe he'd seen something. But right when the breakup was happening, Naade was heading into the restroom. Thankfully, he remembered to hit the privacy setting, and the video went out, but apparently there was a slight glitch in the code, because the audio was still recording. Efi hit the mute on her tablet in time to stave off what she thought would be the worst of the day's footage, but she was so, so wrong. The worst part by far was sifting through hours and hours of tedium in search of that perfect nugget of gossip. There was the gum smacking. The hair twirling. The toe tapping. The mouth breathing. A thousand little irritants the Junie's microphones and cameras picked up.

This definitely wasn't the best use of Efi's time. Efi went online looking for algorithms to do the data sorting for her. She wanted to create something that would skip the boring parts and put all the juicy bits in a nice montage she could watch on the tram ride home from school.

She was browsing the posts on Free Thinkers, the site where she got most of her open source code, when she saw an announcement for a new grant for roboticists. Everyone in the forum discussion was excited about it. It paid a decent amount of naira. Efi knew better than to get her hopes up, but she couldn't help but think about what that kind of money could do. She could upgrade her computers, make them state-of-the-art, so she wouldn't spend as much time twiddling her thumbs while her code compiled. Maybe she could even purchase a model with advanced AI.

Efi clicked the details of the grant, and the normal stipulations applied—for teachers only. Efi sighed. There were dozens of grants listed on the site, but it seemed Efi never met all the qualifications. Sometimes she was too young. Sometimes she didn't have the fancy degrees required. Sometimes her robot-making business was too small. Or too big. There was always *something* holding her back.

Just as Efi was about to log out in frustration, the mail icon on her screen lit up. She opened the inbox and saw a new message sitting there.

From: Anonymous088503

Subject: You've been nominated for the Adawe Foundation Fellowship

Ha. Right. Efi didn't click on it. Probably all kinds of malware and viruses buried in that message. Efi was more than aware of the Adawe Foundation's "Genius Grant"—one of the most prestigious in the world, given in recognition of a person's scientific accomplishments. It was set up in honor of Gabrielle Adawe, a founder of Numbani. There were few people Efi admired more. Last year, she made a diorama in history class on how Adawe had helped create Overwatch, an organization of heroes who worked to end the Omnic Crisis and keep the peace. It was an assignment Efi was rather proud of, despite her dreadful crafting skills. She much preferred wires and circuit boards over construction paper and glue sticks, but even so, her diorama was brilliant. It showed Adawe when she was under-secretary-general of the United Nations, her fist held high as she hailed the original members of Overwatch: Jack Morrison, Gabriel Reyes, Ana Amari, Torbjörn Lindholm, and Reinhardt Wilhelm, among others. It inspired Efi to know that an African woman—a woman whose roots were buried in the same rich soil as Efi's—had more than likely brought the world back from the brink of destruction. Adawe was a hero. Efi would give anything to be nominated for the grant.

That made this fake nomination cut so much deeper. Efi clicked on the message out of spite. She'd scrub her tablet for viruses when she got home. Giving this "anonymous" user a piece of her mind would be worth the risk.

But inside, the message was professional. None of the usual scam markers of a 419 operator. No plea for credit card or bank info. It went into detail about some of Efi's robotic inventions, and how she was being nominated for her ingenuity in helping her community, as well as her potential to achieve even greater feats. It encouraged her to apply for the grant and had a single link at the bottom. Not altered or spoofed. It went directly to an encrypted page on the Adawe Foundation's website. Below the link, the message was simply signed: "A fan."

Efi's hands trembled as she stared at the application form. Was this real? Had someone actually nominated her? Who? "A fan." Did that mean one of her Hollagram followers?

Slowly, Efi composed herself. She would make Adawe proud, using that money to expand her Junie operation and hire help, upgrade the holoimages to use hard-light technology so the robots would be more than just virtual presences—they could assist elderly and disabled people in their homes, too. Her mind was spinning with the possibilities.

She'd have her parents help put together the application this week. Efi looked down the page and saw the deadline in big red letters.

It was due today.

At midnight.

Why hadn't this nomination come sooner? Why at the last minute? Well, better late than not at all. Efi couldn't pass this chance up. She looked at the clock on her tablet as the tram pulled up to her stop. It was 4:10 p.m. That meant she had less than eight hours to fill out the application and write a personal essay. She could do it. Plenty of time.

"Efi!" came her father's voice as soon as she was settled at her laptop and had gotten a few of the application questions answered. "Come set the table. It's time for dinner."

Efi gritted her teeth. Dinner. She rushed through her meal as fast as she could, stuffing beef stew and mixed greens in her mouth and talking at the same time. Pieces of jollof rice flew out as she answered her father's questions. "School was fine. Homework is done. Room is clean. Everything is great!"

"Slow down, dear. You're going to choke on your food," Dad said, tilting his head down so that he could see Efi over the rims of his glasses. He had just arrived home and was still in professor mode, looking every bit the part of in his maroon agbada, a loose robe with detailed embroidery meandering down the lapel.

"Tell us how your robot project is going," Mother said before taking a bite of greens. She chewed slowly, inspecting Efi. Mother was like a superhero when it came to sensing when there was something wrong. So Efi was extra careful not to let on that the fate of the rest of her life was hinging on getting this application turned in on time.

"We've shipped some of the orders already," Efi replied. "Should have the rest done before the month is out."

"That's wonderful. Maybe we can go out to a fancy restaurant the following weekend to celebrate? Hassana and Naade are welcome to come along."

"I'd love that, Mama. But word is spreading about the Junies. We'll have more orders coming in. And I'm already buried with update 3.4. Maybe later?"

Mother sighed, opened her mouth, then closed it again. Efi already knew what she was going to say. That Efi needed to spend more time being a kid. And Mother already knew what Efi would say back, that this *was* her being a kid. A kid who liked building robots more than anything else.

"Okay, maybe after," Mother said, getting up to fetch the dessert from the kitchen. Efi tried to concentrate on enjoying her meal, but the seconds kept ticking by and the pit kept growing in her stomach. She needed to get that grant application in tonight.

"Come on, out with it," her father said once her mother had left the room. "What's going on?"

"Nothing important."

"Honey, you're *always* doing something important. What is it this time?"

"Well, there's a grant I'd like to apply for. A 'Genius Grant' from the Adawe Foundation."

"Wow. That's a big deal!"

"I know. One hundred million naira paid out over five years," Efi said, the amount sounding like an impossibility to her ears. "It'll give me the freedom to really pursue being a roboticist."

"Is there anything I can do to help? Double-check your application form? Proofread your essay? Anything?"

"Can you tell Mama that I excused myself from dessert?" Efi couldn't bear to deal with the disappointment on her mother's face when she told her that she didn't have time for her famous fried plantains.

Dad grimaced. "I suppose I can. But you're sure you don't have any *i*'s that need dotting? Or any *t*'s that need crossing?"

"I'm sure, Dad." Efi smiled at him, and he nodded at her, excusing his daughter. She stepped away quickly and quietly so that her mother wouldn't hear, then proceeded to her room. Efi pulled her laptop into her bed and began to write her essay on how she planned to change the world with this grant money. She typed a few sentences, then deleted them.

Typed more. Deleted them. She knew in her heart what she wanted to say, but putting it into words seemed like an insurmountable task. She started to doubt herself. Yes, she was gifted in science and math, but she was just starting to learn about writing persuasive papers in language arts. There was no way she'd be able to compete with the other nominees and their fancy thesaurus words.

Then Efi had an idea. She had her own following on Hollagram, the social media hub for creators to connect with their supporters. Efi's followers loved her holovid journals, and her updates always got tons of likes and comments. She scanned the application's rules about essays—nothing there indicated the essay had to be *written*. In her vlog posts, she was good at selling robots; now she just had to figure out how to sell herself.

First step, figuring out what to wear. She looked down at her Overwatch pajamas. They were quirky, and she loved them and what they stood for—being a hero—but it wasn't quite the look she was going for. She glanced at the clock on her laptop. 10:30 p.m. She had barely an hour and a half to get this right. She dug through her closet, tossing outfits this way and that. She tried on the black dress with gold foil printed on the fabric, and a couple of chunky loop necklaces, one braided red leather and the other gold. She looked . . . *stylish*. Maybe a little too stylish.

She ditched the dress and tried on a lime-green iro—a stretch of fabric that tied around her waist—and put on the matching short-sleeved buba. The iro was smallish, from a couple of seasons ago, but she loved it, and it was the only thing Efi owned that Hassana had ever complimented. She'd said it reminded her of the bold fabrics that Agba Aja would wear. Being compared to one of the most accomplished Nigerian artists, and an omnic to boot, gave Efi the boost of confidence that she'd need for showing her best side to the Adawe Foundation.

Efi finished the look by adorning her face with white paint that popped against the rich brown of her skin. She hesitated, wondering if using ancestral paint was too much for a grant application, but then remembered the power of story. For Efi, her paint told the story of her people's history and also their future . . . at least the unified future that she imagined for them. Efi knew that was worth going to battle for.

She nodded at herself in the mirror. She looked creative, but perhaps a little too put together. Efi wanted something that said she was not afraid to get her hands dirty.

She flung off the buba but left the green iro hanging off-kilter from her waist.

She didn't have a whole lot of time to spare, but she ran down to her workshop anyway and grabbed her simple white work shirt, toolbelt, and gloves. This look said:

Stylish.

Creative.

Grease-under-the-fingernails.

But tech-savvy. She'd forgotten about tech-savvy. She overturned her peripherals bin on the floor beside her laptop station and found the headset she'd used for gaming, back before her workshop sucked up all her time. It was a modded set. She'd soldered on the loops and horn adornments herself and had added a golden crown after she'd beaten *Vivi's Adventure* on hard mode without any extra lives.

Efi sprinted back to her room and dumped out her entire sock drawer to get her lucky armband, the one her grandfather had worn during the Omnic Crisis. It had seen him through many close calls, and Efi needed all the help she could get.

She gave herself a quick glance in the mirror. Yes, now it was perfect.

Then, at the bottom of her old toy chest, she found Sparky Bot.

She angled the camera on her laptop just right, then pressed RECORD.

"My name is Efi Oladele, and this is Sparky Bot," Efi said, "a fully functioning drone. I made her when I was four years old. She was the first robot of many. I built her to stack block towers nearly up to the ceiling and give my dolls a ride around my play-room. A couple of years later, I built Chore Bot to help my family around the house with cleaning. Ever since I was little, I saw how robots could be more than fun playthings. I learned that they could assist people, and I saw the bond that could form between human and machine.

"Soon after, I started building bots for my neighbors. Like when Mrs. Eni's mother got sick, and she needed someone to watch her cats while she was going back and forth between Numbani and Lagos all the time. I created a robot just for her. It kept her cats fed and watered but didn't stop there. It also played with them—the built-in laser pointer was highly praised—and petted them and called all their names. Mrs. Eni said the robot saved her furniture from becoming scratching posts, too.

"Also, several local high schools are using my hydration robots for their football teams. The robots use facial recognition and medical sensors to make sure each athlete is drinking enough water, and they warn coaches when signs of heat stroke are detected. Wins are up and injuries are down. You know what they say . . . The best offense is a good defense, and the best defense is a hydration robot on the sidelines.

"And now, here's my latest invention." Efi held up the Junie. "The Junior Assistant, or Junie for short. Each Junie is capable of complex navigation and comes equipped with cameras that capture footage in 360 degrees. A built-in AI component can also do research, form opinions, and help the user plan and execute daily tasks."

Efi set the Junie down, letting it walk across the tabletop. "Their main function is to help someone be in multiple places at once. The Junie can project interactive, holographic images of people over great distances, so they can stay in touch and not miss out. It is ideal for workers or students who need to take sick days, but think of all the good this invention could do for chronically ill and disabled people, for people serving in the military, for those working two jobs, or for new parents juggling lots of responsibilities."

Efi pressed the button on the Junie's back, and it projected a 3-D holoimage of her. Efi-Junior pulled up schematics of the bot as well as some blueprints of her plans for further upgrades while the real Efi continued. "Right now I've got more Junie orders than I can process, so I know they're going to fulfill an urgent need. And what comes after this, I'm not quite sure yet, but I do know that I want to continue creating things that could really help my community. I want to solve problems around the world, too, like Gabrielle Adawe did when she helped to establish Overwatch, make peace after the Omnic Crisis, and found Numbani, a city where humans and omnics live together as equals. I want to follow in Adawe's footsteps someday . . . to be a hero. I've got great ideas and big dreams, and with the right support, that someday could be today. I hope you'll consider me for the Adawe Foundation's 'Genius Grant.' I won't let you down."

Efi stopped the recording, then set to editing it. 11:03 p.m. Not much time for anything besides the basics: a slide-in title, a little inspiring music in the background, an aerial shot of Numbani toward the end, and then fade to black. She worked in some footage from her vlog that she'd taken previously of the Junies and her other inventions, too. Some of the video was a little amateurish, but she hoped it made her look more scrappy than sloppy.

A knock came at her door. Efi threw herself under the covers, laptop and all, and pretended to snore. *Please don't be Mama. Please don't be Mama*, she thought.

"Honey?" whispered her mother through the door. "Your lights are on. Why are you still up at this hour?"

The knob turned when Efi didn't answer. She heard her mother stepping softly across the bedroom floor and felt her pulling her covers back. "Efi," Mother said. Efi's snores weren't fooling anyone.

Efi peeled open one eye. She expected to see her mother's stern face, but instead, her mother was smiling and holding a plate piled high with dodo—golden-brown plantain slices that smelled so amazing, Efi had a hard time keeping the saliva in her mouth.

"Your father told me about the grant," Mother said, setting the plate on Efi's dresser.

"He did?"

"I think it's a wonderful opportunity."

"You do?"

"Of course! I know we don't always see eye to eye, but your father and I support you. We're behind you for every single grant you want to apply for."

Efi wanted to smile, though she had a strong feeling a "but" was coming.

"But, honey, I worry about you. And your friends. And rushing through dinner like that—you need to take time to enjoy your family as well."

"I do, Mama. I just . . ." Efi still didn't have the words. She knew that her mother supported her dreams, but often it felt like Efi was living her life for the both of them.

Her mother had been around Efi's age when the first omnic assaults started. Mother didn't talk about those years much, but Efi knew that time was scary beyond anything she could imagine. Mother simply wanted Efi not to miss out on the parties, the friends, the fun and carefree days that the Omnic Crisis had stolen from her. Efi bashfully took a fried plantain from the plate, resisting the urge to stuff the whole thing in her mouth. Instead, she took a dainty bite and savored it. Still hot. Mother must have made a new batch just for her. For a moment, Efi completely put the application deadline out of her mind. Her mother pulled her close and kissed her on the forehead.

"Mama, I promise if I get this grant, I'll take some time to slow down. Maybe we could go on a family vacation."

That perked her mother up. "Oh, Efi! That would be wonderful. We could go relax on the beaches in Lagos or visit Yankari National Park to see the elephants and hippos. It'd be so nice to get some time away. Somewhere we can all unplug. You get the grant, and we'll go. Your choice."

"Thanks, Mama," Efi said, snuggling into her mother's side. Mother gently tugged at the ends of Efi's hair twists, making sure they were lying just right.

"So what are you and your friends up to these days?"

"You mean besides robots?" Efi asked.

"Including robots," Mother said. "I want to hear all the good bits."

"Well, Naade hasn't been caught dancing in the hallways between classes this week. He taught his Junie to whistle whenever it sees a teacher coming."

"Ha! Why am I not surprised?"

Their time together lasted only a few minutes, but in between bites, Efi took this opportunity to tell her mother everything that had been on her mind lately. Her mother nodded and listened, oohed and aahed in all the right spots when Efi brought up her recent frustrations. Efi felt heard and loved and understood, and it was over all too quickly.

"Brush your teeth. Clean your room," Mother said as she left. Then she winked at Efi. "Don't stay up past midnight."

Efi nodded, then engaged Chore Bot. It came to life and started raking up her socks and folding her clothes. It tried to make the bed with Efi still in it, but she dismissed it back to its corner. Efi put the finishing touches on her video, then added one more line.

"I want to change the world and make it a better place for my friends. And my family."

There. Not perfect, but if the board at the Adawe Foundation could look an almost twelve-year-old with a dream like that in the eye and not want to help her, then there was no hope for anyone.

She was almost positive she would win that grant.

Now she just had to wait to find out for sure.

HollaGram

HOLOVID TRANSCRIPT
Automatically Generated by TranscriptMinderXL version 5.317

Application for the Adawe Foundation "Genius Grant"

I can't believe it. I just submitted my application for the Adawe Foundation's "Genius Grant" with three minutes to spare. I love creating robots for you all, and I'm super excited for what's going to happen next!

Imagine what I could do with that sort of money. Anybody interested in hard-light upgrades for their Junie?!?!

It's so late. I'm so tired.

REACTIONS

 247 👏289 📣229

COMMENTS (37)

ARTIST4Life Efi! Is that my fave green iro you're wearing? Love your new look so much! (Let me borrow that gold necklace tho.)

BackwardsSalamander I vote for hard-light upgrades. Then my Junie could help me around the house. LOVING it, by the way! I call mine Penelope.

BolajiOladele55 This is your dad. Go to sleep.

Read more . . .

CHAPTER 3

Efi used her last few moments before her friends got dismissed from school to review the condensed video feed of the day's events. Friday's was a full twenty-two minutes long, which meant there was a lot of juicy stuff going on, but Efi nearly bit her tongue when she watched Stevie Igwe getting his hand caught in the Zobo Bot's dispenser. The Zobo Bot was known to be ornery, taking its dear, sweet time when making juice drinks. But the ingredients were fresh, with the most fragrant hibiscus leaves, and the students enjoyed watching as the automatic knives sliced up pieces of pineapple and ginger right before their eyes. Efi didn't know what Stevie had been thinking, but instead of waiting for the drink bottle to dispense, he'd shoved his hand up inside the bot and was stuck like that until a teacher came to rescue him.

The new Junie algorithms Efi had set up were working perfectly, and she felt like she was at school with her friends all day. Even Hassana and Naade had stopped complaining and were fully embracing the technology, both in and out of school. Word was spreading rapidly about Efi's invention, and a hundred more Junie orders had come in just this week! Keeping busy was such a distraction that Efi had barely noticed that it'd been just over a month since she submitted her grant application. Thirty-six and a half days. Eight hundred and seventy-nine hours. Who was counting?

Finally, the school bell rang, and Efi stood up on her tiptoes, looking for her friends to come rushing out. They had big plans this weekend: lots of workshop time, but she planned to play movies in the background as they assembled robots. Real movies, like *Flash Brighton and the Omnic Crusaders: The Duel to Infinity*, starring Kam Kalu, Thespion 4.0, A.I. Schylus, and about two dozen other popular actors, both human and omnic. If Efi had a naira for every time Naade raved about that movie, her entire workshop would be funded for eternity, and she'd never have to worry over getting grants again.

"Naade!" Efi said, waving her hands. "Over here!"

Naade saw her and his eyes lit up as he came sauntering over. Hassana followed not far behind.

"Did you see it?" Hassana said. "Stevie versus the Zobo Bot?"

"It was so ridiculous!" Efi said. "He should have been patient and waited for his drink like everyone else. He definitely 'pulled an Isaac' with that one."

Naade laughed. "Yeah, he did. Learned his lesson the hard way for sure! Lọ lati sun pẹlu apọju apọju, ji soke pẹlu ọwọ wiwọ."

Efi nodded and laughed at the old proverb, but Hassana just

stood there, eyes squinting, like she was searching for a translation in the little bit of Yoruba she knew.

"It means 'Go to sleep with an itchy butt, wake up with a stinky hand,'" Naade offered.

"Ew, Naade," Hassana said, lips curled. "Way too much information."

"What? Oh, no . . . I didn't . . ." Naade said, stumbling over his words. "It's just something my dad always says to me. About how a little problem can lead to a bigger problem if you let it, or something. I promise it's much more elegant in Yoruba."

"Naade, don't ever change," Efi said, smiling. "So are we all excited for this weekend?"

"Yeah, about that . . ." Hassana said, her smile suddenly fading. She unzipped her backpack, took the Junie out, and handed it to Efi.

"What? Is it malfunctioning? I'll take a look when we get back to the workshop."

"No! It works great. It was a lifesaver on Wednesday. I sent it to choir practice while I was at my art competition. I would have missed out completely if I hadn't had it."

Efi stood there silently and waited for the other shoe to drop.

Hassana shook her head, gritted her teeth, and said, "But, I'm sort of double-booked for tonight. I forgot I promised Amber that I'd help her find some outfits for the Unity Day festivities. I was hoping I could send the Junie with you and Naade, so at least I'd be there in spirit?"

"*Ooooo*," Naade said, handing his Junie to Efi as well. "I actually can't make it tonight, either. But my Junie can."

"Are you double-booked, too?" Efi said, only mildly annoyed. But it was growing. Fast.

"I guess you could sort of say that . . . I'm grounded."

"What'd you do this time, Naade?" Hassana asked.

"Well," Naade said. "I'd been thinking of what Efi said about taking my studies seriously, so I came up with a plan. I had my Junie record all my classes, right? So I thought, why not use my time more efficiently? I could do my math homework during history. My history homework in science lab. My science lab homework in language arts. Then when I got home, most of my homework would be done already, which would leave more time for me to play *Vivi's Adventure*. Brilliant, right?"

"But when did you find time to go over the feeds from your classes?" Efi asked.

"That's the best part. You know how, in science lab, we learned about osmosis? Breaking down the barriers between molecules so they can move freely?"

"That's not what osmosis is," Efi said, but Naade was in the zone and just kept talking.

"So I had this idea, see: Why couldn't I learn by osmosis? Information breaking through the barrier . . . of sleep?"

"That's *really* not how—"

"And each night I played the recordings while I slept. And with seven hours of class, and eight hours of sleep, it worked out perfectly, plus I had an hour to spare. I played the recordings again at ten times speed, just to make sure everything sunk in." Naade tapped his head.

"Okay, now you're being ridic—"

"But something must have gone wrong with your tech, Efi, because these past couple weeks, my grades have been getting worse and worse. I brought home a D on my math quiz, and that was the final straw for my dad. Grounded. But take my Junie with you. Maybe see if you can find the bugs. In the meantime, I guess I'll have to go back to studying the old-fashioned way." His shoulders slumped.

"Yeah, I'll see what I can do," Efi said. She didn't have the heart to tell him the truth: that his plan was possibly the worst she'd ever heard. But she could stall and stall and keep his Junie locked up in her workshop until Naade's grades had time to recover.

Hassana winked at Efi. "You're a good friend."

Efi managed to smile, but that didn't make the twenty-minute ride home on the tram any less lonely. About halfway there, she saw something flicker out of the corner of her eye. She pressed closer to the window and saw at least a dozen OR15 robots marching their four-legged march on patrol around the city's center. They were built like centaurs, their matte-gray titanium frame covered with polished white chest plating and green plating on four hulking legs. She liked the way they moved together—like show ponies, almost prancing. Massive, heavily armed, and highly lethal show ponies. It seemed like there were more on the street than usual, doing their job of keeping the peace.

Efi appreciated the security work the OR15s did, but she sort of wished someone would give the entire fleet a nice upgrade to bring them closer to Numbani's aesthetic. They were sleeker than the old OR14 "Idina" models that served during the Omnic Crisis for sure, but Efi always felt like the robots were missing crucial pieces of Numbani heritage. They were intimidating. Terse. They never bowed to show respect and never used honorifics. Efi hated to say it, but the OR15s had that "straight out of the box" attitude, more focused on catching criminals than they were on integrating into the community. If Efi could have a crack at their programming, she'd make changes so they could fully serve and protect the citizens of Numbani. The OR15s could be the type of heroes that were just as eager to assist the elderly as they were to nullify terrorists. Just as comfortable reading library books to kids as they were battling Talon agents. Efi's head started swelling with ideas, but a jolt from the tram startled her back to reality.

Efi didn't have any business trying to figure out how to better integrate the OR15s. She had enough problems of her own already. Her Junie production was still running behind, and she really needed to get that grant money. She logged on to the Adawe Foundation's grant website and checked her status:

PENDING . . .

She refreshed the page once. Twice. By the time she got home, she must have hit that button a hundred times.

Don't obsess, she said to herself. She went to her workshop, then activated both Naade's and Hassana's Junies to keep her company. The holoimages stood there, looking at her. Blank stares. Blank smiles. They filled the workshop with nothing but coldness. She turned them off, then got to work.

Ding. Ding. Ding, her laptop chirped out. More orders.

Efi sighed, opened a new box of Lúcio-Oh's, cranked the music to volume ten, and fired up her solder gun.

Efi stood in the hallway after her calculus class let out and scrolled through Hassana's feed on Hollagram. There had to be at least three dozen selfies of Hassana goofing off with Amber Oyeba, the coolest girl in their school. They'd gone clothes shopping together, Amber's arm hanging over Hassana's shoulder, fancy Aetria shopping bags in their hands. Big, giant smiles on both their faces.

Would have invited you, her message had said to Efi. *But we knew you were busy with the bots all weekend.*

"Why so long in the face?" Dayo said, suddenly standing next to Efi. She realized the hallways had completely emptied. How long had she been standing there?

"Friend drama," Efi said to her cousin.

"Wanna talk about it?"

"Not especially. I need to go. I'm probably already late for my tram."

"Wait," Dayo said. "Why don't you stay after for drama club? You can help us build sets for the Unity Day play."

"Ehhh . . ." She'd *literally* be watching paint dry. "Pass."

"Come on, Efi. You can make friends here if you try. A couple of them think you're cool."

Efi perked up. "They think I'm cool?"

"Genius. Inventor. Entrepreneur. Social activist. What's not cool about you?"

"I guess I can stay for a bit," Efi said.

Dayo pumped a fist in the air, then led her down the hall to the theater. Efi could smell the paint and sawdust as soon as he opened the door. On the stage, a dozen students were working feverishly on props and set pieces.

He walked Efi halfway down the center aisle to where Sam was working with a girl Efi hadn't met before, tall and thin with long arms that looked like they were perfect for reaching up into high cabinets. She wore a colorful hijab loose over her hair, the end of the scarf dangling perilously close to the paint bucket.

"Efi, you remember Sam," Dayo said. "And this is Joké, our stage manager. Efi's going to be helping us out today."

"Awesome," Joké said. "It's nice to meet you. I'd shake your hand, but . . ." She presented Efi with her paint-covered palms.

"It's going to be epic," Dayo said. "All of the stage props are being upcycled from found objects. The Harmony Key that Gabrielle Adawe presented to the leader of the Numbani Omnic Union is made from pool noodles. And you won't believe what the Doomfist gauntlet is made of."

"Don't talk about Doomfist," Sam said, looking up from his project to give Dayo a sneer. "You'll scare the kid!"

"I'm not scared of Doomfist," Efi said. She wasn't excited

about being referred to as "the kid," either. She did remember some about what Doomfist had done, though. Her parents had tried to shield her from the worst of the atrocities committed by Akinjide Adeyemi, the Scourge of Numbani, but it was difficult to ignore, especially for someone as good at putting together puzzles as she was.

She remembered their "Super Fun Family Time" game, when Efi and her parents would drop everything and rush into the interior bathroom of their flat over the blare of warning sirens. There was a small box they kept in there, full of bubbles and modeling clay and the sugary snacks her parents usually forbade Efi to eat. They even let her watch Overwatch cartoons back-to-back-to-back, the volume on her tablet cranked as high as it would go. But even with all those wonderfully fun distractions, Efi never felt at ease during those times. Maybe it was the fear hiding at the edges of her father's smile. Maybe it was the way her mother hugged her just a little too tightly. Maybe it was the thundering sounds of buildings crumbling in the distance in the brief silence before a commercial break. She'd willed herself not to be scared, so her parents would have one less thing to worry about, and that fearlessness just sort of stuck.

Efi shook off the tainted memory and squinted at the gauntlet prop: a big, bold fist painted gold with metal spikes sticking out from the knuckles. She didn't have any experience building props out of trash, but she had a knack for reverse-engineering technology. She looked at the gauntlet with her mind's eye, tracing the lines and angles. Finally, it hit her—looking at the segments and the organic shape with little prongs wrapping under the arm.

"That's the giant plastic lobster that used to hang above the seafood section at Bankolé's Grocery!"

"You guessed it!" Dayo said. "We rearranged the pincers to make the fingers like an oversized glove. I knew you'd fit right in. You're well on your way to becoming a theater geek."

"I'm just glad Numbani is peaceful again," said Joké. "It's nice that my biggest worry now is which one of you is going to mess up your lines on opening night." She squinted hard at Sam.

"What?" Sam said innocently. "It's not my fault villains like to break out into lengthy monologues. I'll have it memorized by Unity Day, I swear. I'll be the best Doomfist anyone's ever seen!"

Joké shook her head and raised a brow at Efi, like she was asking *Can you believe this guy?*

Efi smiled, feeling a little more confident about hanging out with Dayo, Sam, Joké, and the other drama students.

"You wanna help assemble the bars for Doomfist's cell?" Sam asked her.

"Actually, Doomfist's prison cell is made from meter-thick solid—" Efi stopped herself when she noticed a frown forming on Sam's face. She bit her lip. Did it really matter how accurate the play was? That scourge, Akinjide Adeyemi, was dead, and Akande Ogundimu, his successor, was locked away for good. The havoc the two Doomfists had inflicted upon Numbani was history. "Sure, I'd love to help make bars," Efi said as she sat down next to Sam, a bunch of paper towel rolls and aluminum foil at their feet.

"It's super simple. Just take three rolls and put them end to end. Add a little tape to hold them in place, then wrap the foil around, and ta-da, a set of impenetrable prison bars. And all I had to do was raid the school bathrooms for two months straight!"

"Well, I certainly feel safe with Doomfist caught behind those!" Efi said with an awkward laugh. She loved the simplicity of the design. She made seven of them, listening to Sam, Dayo, and Joké talk. She paid close attention to the words they used—lots of theater slang, but she mostly kept up. Maybe she could fit in, if she tried really hard.

"You know what I love most about Unity Day?" Efi asked. "The festival food! Especially the meat pies and the egg rolls and the boiled peanuts. And don't forget the kuli-kuli!" Efi's mouth started to water over those deep-fried treats, best eaten when there was still a chance of them burning your tongue.

"Oh, yeah, those are so good. And I start shaking as soon as I hear the coconut candy vendor hollering up and down the street, tossing bags into the crowd," said Sam, looking forlornly at his paint-stained hands. "And your fingers get all sticky and covered in caramel, and you just have to lick them. Even if your parents give you *that look*."

Efi nodded, a big grin stretched across her face. Sticky fingers were a universal experience during Unity Day, celebrating harmony and equality between humans and omnics, who had their own set of indulgences. Organic oils were poured into wineglasses and OmniWorx synthetic greases came packaged in designer tins, smelling of mint or lavender or citrus blends. Efi always put aside a little of her money to buy a few tins for the special omnics in her life—teachers, neighbors, and friends—and in truth, the appreciation they showed her in return made her feel much better than having a stomach full of greasy food.

Unity Day was only a month away now, and Efi couldn't wait. She sang the Numbani Harmony Anthem to herself as she worked. Dayo joined in. They were less than harmonic . . . Vocal skills didn't run very deep in their family, but Sam and Joké picked up the slack and brought the song to life until Dayo tried to hit that high note at the end with an off-pitch falsetto that made Efi's molars hurt.

Efi winced at Dayo, and he smiled back.

You're doing great, he mouthed at her.

Sam counted up the prison bars and deemed there were enough. "Amazing job," he said to Efi. "Dayo is so lucky to have an awesome cousin like you."

Efi looked at Sam and smiled, but then she saw his hand coming down toward her head. She had half a second to react. Of all the things she hated most, it was being patted on the head. She couldn't let him make her look more like a child. She didn't want to embarrass herself in front of Dayo's crew, either. But her ego won out, and Efi stuck her hand up and caught Sam by the wrist.

"Do I look like a poodle?" she asked him.

"No," he said.

"A cocker spaniel?"

"No."

"A Labrador retriever?"

"No."

"Then please do not pet me." She said this in her most stern, grown-up voice. The students all started laughing and pointing at Sam, yelling at him that he'd been told off by a kid. He was the one they were teasing, but Efi felt the sting of being different as well. She was a kid, yes, but it felt like more of a part-time thing . . . Except when the older students laughed.

She didn't need this. "Well, anyway, I've got to get going. Sorry I won't be able to make it to your play, but I'll be out of town. On vacation for the whole week of Unity Day celebrations." She nodded to herself. Her parents had said they would take her on a vacation if she got that grant.

Yes, she still hadn't heard back yet, but in that moment she was feeling confident. Really confident.

"Ooh, vacation? Where to?" Dayo asked. "Why didn't Auntie mention it?"

"Because it's big. It's huge. She didn't want to sound like she was bragging."

"Your mother? Not bragging to mine? Ha!"

"Well, she didn't because—because . . ." Efi fished for something. Anything. And then she remembered Lúcio's concert tour schedule. She practically had it tattooed to the backs of her eyelids when it was first announced. She and Hassana had wept into bowls of chocolate ice cream when they saw he wasn't stopping in Numbani until the very end of his tour, still nearly eight months away. They'd stood in the virtual ticket line anyway, to no avail. It sold out in less than twenty-seven minutes. But fortunately, Lúcio's concert in his home town of Rio de Janeiro was one of the last few venues that still had tickets available. A thousand fourteen seats, as of this morning.

Not that Efi checked *every* morning.

"We're seeing Lúcio. In Brazil!" she shouted.

"Whoa!" Sam said. "Sick!"

They all started crowding around her. "Where are you staying?"

"When are you leaving?"

"Who are you going with?"

The questions kept coming. Why had she said that? She didn't even know if she'd gotten the grant yet, and even if she did get it, she knew her parents wouldn't spring for a trip across the ocean!

Efi looked at Dayo for help, but he just stared back and shrugged. She'd dug herself too deep of a hole with this one. "My tram! Sorry, I've got to catch the last one before rush hour, or I'll never get a seat!"

And then she was off, the stench of her big lie chasing after her through the vacant school hallways. Evening was nearing, and as safe as Numbani was, it made her nervous to go out by herself. She looked back, relieved that Dayo was following her.

58

But he didn't look upset. Quite the opposite. His smile was as wide and friendly as it had ever been.

"Efi," he said, sounding so much like Auntie Yewande whenever Efi found herself getting a talking-to on one of her visits to their house. It happened more often than Efi wanted to admit. "Things kind of got out of hand back there, didn't they?"

He set both of his hands on the crystal knob of his cane, then leaned into her ever so slightly. The bend in his brow was definitely Auntie Yewande's. Efi didn't know if it was genetic or learned, but that bend had a special power of dragging the truth out of wayward children. And it was working, dang it, because next thing Efi knew, her mouth was open, and she was babbling like a brook.

"I'm sorry I made all of that up back there. I hope I didn't embarrass you. I just wanted to seem cool. They keep looking at me like I'm a baby!"

"I'll talk to them. They didn't mean any harm by it, but I get your point. It's no fun to be the odd one out. Come back in. Let's get finished up, and then we can ride home together."

"I can't go back in there. Not after that mess I said about going to Brazil!"

"Just tell them the truth. They'll understand. Heh, you probably don't remember, but when I was not much older than you, I used to go around telling people that my father belonged to Overwatch and was best buds with Reinhardt, but he was deep, deep, deep undercover so no one had ever heard of him."

Efi laughed. She vaguely remembered it. He'd shown her his

father's "secret Overwatch medallion." It'd been made of several layers of very carefully cut Nano Cola cans and smelled of the entire bottle of clear fingernail polish he'd used to make it glossy. Efi guessed that Dayo had always been good at crafting things out of junk.

"Does that mean you'll come back in? Maybe they can find you a part in the play."

Efi was willing to give it another try. She'd bring them some packages of chin chin next time she came to smooth things over. She'd noticed the students here were partial to the mega-lemon flavor, though she couldn't understand why. They were so tart, they made Efi's lips curl when she crunched into them. But as soon as Efi opened her mouth to accept the offer, her tablet alerted her with a ring. She looked down at the notification on the screen.

Message from: Adawe Foundation

Subject: Your Application Status

Efi's heart nearly stopped. So soon?

"What is it?" asked Dayo. "You look like you've seen a ghost."

"It's that 'Genius Grant.' They've made a decision!"

"And?" Dayo said excitedly. "What's it say?"

"I don't know. I can't look." She shoved her tablet at her cousin. "Here. You open it."

Dayo timidly reached for the tablet, but then Efi snatched it back. "No. I'll look." She took another deep breath. "I don't want to know. No, wait. I do. Here . . ." she said, handing it to him.

He didn't reach out to take it.

"I'm serious. I want you to open it," Efi said bashfully.

Finally, Dayo took it, clicked on the screen, and started reading. To himself.

"Well?" Efi practically screamed. She felt so nervous, like she was about to crawl out of her skin.

"It says, 'Efi, have you considered refinancing your home loan? Rates now are at a historic—'"

"Not that message! Here, give it to me."

Dayo handed the tablet back with a smirk. Efi's finger trembled as it hit the link. She feverishly scanned over the first couple of lines:

Efi Oladele, congratulations! You've been selected as this year's recipient of the Adawe Foundation Fellowship—

Things started to get dizzy. Then Efi saw all those zeroes at the end of her grant money, and she had to sit down right there on the tile floor.

"I'm assuming this is a good scream?" Dayo shouted.

Was she screaming? Yes, apparently, she was. So loud, in fact, that all the students from drama club had come out into the hallway.

"What's going on?" Sam asked.

Dayo looked at Efi, pointedly. She was supposed to apologize to them, right? To admit she'd lied, but . . .

But, now that she'd won the award, her parents would take

her on a vacation, and they knew how much she loved Lúcio. And she was off school that week for the Unity celebration, so she wouldn't have to miss any classes. It was all so perfect.

"I'm going to Brazil to see Lúcio!" she shouted at them.

It would happen! There was no way her parents could say no.

HollaGram

FANS **483**

HOLOVID TRANSCRIPT
Automatically Generated by TranscriptMinderXL version 5.317

I WON THE GRANT!!!!

Am I dreaming? I just got news that I've won the grant! I'm filming this holovid on the tram ride home. Can you just look out the window at this wonderful view? Gabrielle Adawe had a vision for creating Overwatch to negotiate peace between humans and omnics and founded this harmonious city that the people of Numbani proudly call home. And now I'm going to be a part of continuing her legacy.

No pressure, though, right?

But first, I'm taking a much-needed vacation. Can't wait to break the news to my parents. I owe them so much! And to the anonymous person who nominated me for the award, whoever you are, wherever you are . . . thank you!

REACTIONS

COMMENTS (98)

NaadeForPrez Congrats, Efi! I knew you could do it. Let's celebrate with puff puffs. You're buying! :)

ARTIST4Life Nice, Naade. Yes, we'll be celebrating. And the puff puffs are on us! As many as you can eat!

BackwardsSalamander Cool! Congrats! Any updates on those hard-light upgrades, though? Penelope keeps asking about them. She's so funny. It's like she's got a mind of her own!

Read more

CHAPTER 4

"Absolutely not," her mother said.

"I don't think you understand," Efi said. "We're off all that week of school. There's a nonstop flight from Numbani to Rio, only four hours. Pricepoint Ticketing has a couple of good deals, if we roll the flights in with the hotel. And once you figure in the exchange rates, it'll be only a little more expensive than if we went to Lagos or the animal reserve."

"Lagos has great music venues," Efi's father said, his nose buried in his tablet. "Looks like Tonal Abyss will be playing that week. Why don't we go there? It's less hassle, and I'm sure you and your friends will have just as much fun as you would at a Lúcio concert."

"Tonal Abyss?" Efi gasped. "They haven't put out a new album since I was seven years old!"

The omnic pop band had thirty-eight members, and at one point, Efi could name every single one of them. Then internal drama broke the band apart—they couldn't decide on a standard measure of time for their music. Constantine, the founder and lead vocalist, preferred Quantum Clock Geneva Time, and Gaxx Gator, the bass player, wanted to switch to Quantum Clock Greenwich Time, which was gaining popularity among some big-name omnic performers. The band had chosen sides, neatly split down the middle, and no one would budge. They'd tried using both timing standards during their performances, but the gravitational time dilations due to different elevations of the clocks threw their synchronicity off so much that they resorted to playing old prerecorded tunes at their concerts.

Efi couldn't tell the difference that microfraction of a microsecond they were arguing about made, but she remembered the omnic community in Numbani being up in arms about it, appalled that Tonal Abyss had lost its mojo. It was about that time when Efi had developed an appreciation for Lúcio's music and started to favor that over those rehashed tunes of her early childhood.

"Please, Daddy? Mummy?" she begged. "You told me I need to do things that kids my age do. Well, kids go to concerts! With their friends. Kids fly across oceans. I've never even been on a plane."

Efi gave her father the pouty eyes. It wouldn't work on her mother, but if she could sway him, at least there'd be a chance.

"I know going to Rio is a hassle compared to staying local," Efi said. "But what if we took the road less traveled by—traversing the great unknown with only the power-core on our backs and the alloy-plating on our feet? We must trek as a family, as we cherish the things that hold us together, so that we will not just fall apart!" Yes, she'd misquoted three of her father's favorite literary icons—Frost, Blanchet771, Achebe—all in one breath, but the stakes were high. "If you decide to take us to Lagos, I know I'll have a great time. But if we go to Rio, right now, when all the stars are lined up . . . we'll have the time of our lives."

Efi's mother and father exchanged looks. They could have an entire conversation with the squints of their eyes and tilts of their heads. Efi thought she might be able to make out the slightest hint of a smile on her mother's face.

Yes. Yes. It was working.

"We will . . . think about it," her mother said, which was practically her screaming *yes* from the rooftops.

Still, Efi didn't want to jinx herself, so she nodded and said, "Thank you for considering it, Mama. I will patiently await your decision."

And then Efi was running to her workshop as fast as she could, mentally packing her best outfits in her head.

For the next few weeks as the trip approached, Efi could hardly contain herself. She was sure there wasn't a person in Numbani who didn't know she was taking her two best friends on a big adventure across the ocean to meet their all-time-favorite hero. And last night, Efi had stayed up double- and triple-checking the details of their itinerary:

MONDAY—Check in to hotel, relax at rooftop pool . . .

TUESDAY—Hard-light skate tour through downtown Rio . . .

WEDNESDAY—Surf lessons at Ipanema, tour botanical gardens . . .

THURSDAY—Favela fundraiser block party, pictures with Lúcio's hologram . . .

FRIDAY—CONCERT!!!

Running on less than two hours of sleep, Efi should be tired, and yet she wasn't. The adrenaline set in as soon as the sunlight cut through the gaps in her curtains. Efi threw them wide, cracked open the window, too, and screamed at the gazelle-headed tower facing her, "Today, I am flying to Rio to see Lúcio in concert!"

The gazelle building stared back at her, like it didn't care. Like this wasn't the absolute best day of Efi's life. She rushed into the clothes she had laid out two days prior, grabbed the suitcase she'd started packing two weeks prior, and picked up the small foil-wrapped present sitting on her dresser.

Her mother stumbled into the living room to greet her

daughter. "Up so early?" she said, wiping the sleep out of her eyes. "Our plane doesn't leave for another nine hours."

"Good morning, Mama," Efi said with a little curtsy. She waited a few giddy moments for her mother to nod and smile, then shoved the present into her hands. "Open it, please."

"Now? Can't it wait until after breakfast?"

Efi shook her head and jumped up and down. She didn't know how much longer she'd be able to contain her excitement. Her father was up, too, now, mumbling something that sounded like "making coffee," but Efi couldn't be sure.

Mother shrugged and then opened the present. Confused, she looked back at Efi.

"Earplugs? I know you think we're old, but your father and I can handle a little loud music. Back in our day—"

"It's not for the music," Efi said. Then the doorbell rang. She could hear Hassana and Naade outside the door chanting "Lúcio! Lúcio!" then screaming loud enough to wake any neighbors that hadn't already been disturbed by Efi's morning crowing. She looked at her parents, and they both took the cue and put in their earplugs. They were polyform-styled silicone, the best money could buy. And Efi's parents were going to need them.

Efi opened the door. The volume got louder, and she and her friends started talking, but all that would come out were shrill noises that only approximated language. Efi had her tablet loaded up with every single one of Lúcio's tracks, ordered by awesomeness, cross indexed by danceability.

Later, they stuffed all their bags into a taxi, and then they were off to the airport. With so many streets shut down for the Unity Day parades, it was difficult to cut across the city. Traffic slowed to a creep. Efi knew they'd left plenty of time to get there, and yet there was a small fear that they'd miss their flight.

Naade rolled down the window, and the smell of hot cooking oil filtered into their car and tempted them to step outside. Not three meters away there was a puff puff vendor selling those golden balls of goodness, stacked high in a pyramid and dusted with powdered sugar. Efi had to pull the back of Naade's shirt to keep him inside the car.

Humans and omnics danced together in a parade that stretched as far down the street as they could see. The drumbeat pounded in Efi's heart, and then her foot was tapping. There'd been some rumors that the event would be postponed due to an anonymous threat, but the citizens of Numbani expressed their outrage and promised to show up in the streets whether the city sanctioned it or not.

Still, there was the faintest shadow of tension cast over the festivities, but Efi couldn't pinpoint what it was. Maybe people's smiles weren't quite as full. Maybe it was how omnics stood ever-so-slightly farther away from humans. Or maybe it was the looming presence of so many security guards, both human and robot, lurking at the outskirts of the festival.

Efi blinked, and then the shadow was gone, and even if tensions were mounting beyond Numbani's borders, that didn't mean they would put a damper on the festivities here. Efi saw some kids her age, smiles on their faces, eyes wide from all the excitement. Their high-pitched voices belted out the Numbani anthem in between sips of their sugar drinks.

Efi hadn't missed a Unity Day celebration since she was born. It was so big, so loud, so colorful that it filled the entire week, and rivaled Carnival Calabar in size. It was Numbani's most important holiday, at least if you ranked holidays by how bad your stomach felt the next morning. She was almost sad she would miss the festivities this year.

Almost.

Naade started beatboxing the bassline of "We Move Together as One" and Hassana tossed in some funky fizz-grind-pop sounds, and all those feelings went away. Efi attempted some synthetic-sounding beats of her own, and they didn't sound half bad. They didn't sound half good, either, but none of that mattered. In exactly ninety-eight hours and twelve minutes, they would be seeing Lúcio, up on the stage, his locs flying as he turned some serious tunes on his tables. The same tunes that helped liberate his favela.

"We should have taken the tram," Efi's father said after a ten-minute stretch of absolute standstill. Above, a tram soared beneath its track, looking like a bird swooping between skyscrapers.

"Driver, can we take the route by the museum?" Mother asked, popping out one of her earplugs, yet leaving it close by in case spontaneous squealing from the back seat broke out yet again.

"Calculating route," the driverless interface said, the

electric-blue light on the dashboard flashing. It beeped a sour note of concern. "That route has a forty-five-minute backup. We're on the fastest route."

"The fastest route would be walking," Naade said, watching as an entire family dressed in matching purple-and-white printed fabrics passed them, including a toddler defiantly pushing her own stroller and a nanny omnic walking a few steps behind, wearing an aso ebi dress that matched the rest of the family. The nanny shook her gleaming metal head in frustration.

"Would you like to disembark?" the driverless interface asked with just a hint of snark.

"Definitely not," Father said. "We'd lose Naade to the first puff puff vendor we passed."

"Oh, Uncle!" Naade gasped, pressing his hand to his chest, feigning insult. "I don't eat puff puff that much!"

"Is that so?" Father asked, pursing his lips. He gestured at Naade with his chin. "Look at you, you eat so much puff puff, you've got it growing out of your ears!"

Naade went silent, and Efi put her hand to her mouth, trying to hold back her laughter for her friend's sake. She'd warned him last week not to touch the plate in the fridge, but the pile of round little dough balls was too high, too tempting. When Father got home and noticed his favorite treat was missing, he got so upset that Efi thought he was going to cancel their whole trip on the spot. Normally, Efi's father was quick to forgive, but Naade had crossed a line.

"Am I wrong?" Father asked. "Or have you forgotten how to speak?"

"No, Uncle," Naade murmured.

This trip promised to be an interesting six days for sure.

"I guess everyone is in town to see Doomfist's gauntlet," Mother said, redirecting the conversation, but her words were curt and oddly emotionless. "There's a new exhibit."

"Who would want to see something that destructive?" Efi asked.

Naade and Hassana raised their hands.

"All that power," Naade was saying as he clenched his fist. "I'd only use it for good, of course!" The smirk on his face said otherwise.

In any case, they got to experience a taste of Unity Day as they slowly wound their way through the city, until finally, they pulled up to the Adawe International Terminal. Security took forever as well. Efi had practically fit a miniature workshop into her carry-on and had to explain why she had three different tablet devices, a Junie, and two laptops. Security kept squinting at her, asking her parents the same five questions over and over, and telling them to boot all the devices up to show that they worked, and weren't weapons of any sort. No one addressed Efi directly, so she played around on one of her laptops, connecting to the airport Wi-Fi so she could check the weather in Rio—sunny and warm, forecasted all throughout the week. She couldn't believe their luck. Then her screen flickered, and the entire webpage shifted sideways a few centimeters, then snapped back in place, leaving a magenta ghost image behind.

Weird.

Efi checked the wireless connections available, and a list popped up. One by one, they blinked out, until there was only one left. 344X-Azúcar. Efi started to click on it, but then Efi's mother's voice reached that octave where someone was about to get a piece of her mind, and Efi stiffened up on instict. By the time Efi realized that for once it wasn't her who was in trouble with her mother, the 344X-Azúcar connection was gone.

Mother may not have been excited about Efi's obsession with robots, but let some stranger imply that her daughter wasn't actually a genius and she had a few choice words for that security officer, for sure. They kept talking over and around Efi, so she tuned them out, watching as a group of OR15s escorted a couple of dignified-looking people wearing Numbani Heritage Museum jackets across the concourse. Behind them floated a transport cart, like the ones you could rent from the airport to help with luggage, but bigger. And instead of holding bags, there was a single large cylinder sitting atop it. Whatever was inside it was hidden beneath heavily tinted glass.

Efi stiffened.

That had to be the Doomfist gauntlet. She was very glad it would soon be protected under twenty centimeters of bullet-proof glass.

Finally, after a very heated discussion, security allowed Efi through with her computers intact. Mother was saying something to her now, in that social-worker voice she used with her clients, about responsibility and expectations, but Efi was so distracted, she only heard every other word. The flickering lights of the departures and arrivals boards had snatched her attention, tracking flights to and from all over the world. Posters for London, Moscow, and Cairo caught her eye, and she was especially taken by the one for Tokyo, with all the pretty cherry blossoms. Next grant she won, she'd definitely get her parents to take her there.

"Efi, why aren't you listening?" her mother asked, snapping fingers in front of Efi's face. Efi came to and saw her mother looking down at her, and though she'd just defended her child with a ferociousness that Efi had never seen, somehow Efi felt that she'd made a mistake.

"Why did you have to bring so much?" her mother asked. "I thought the whole point of this vacation was for you to get away from those robots!"

"Sorry, Mama. But I needed my dev box to code on. And my test box to run my simulations, which means I need to run a Maxwell Interpreter to autosort all eight billion permutations into virtual hash matrices, which means I need a dedicated MI box. Unless you expect me to do all that on my tablet with the preinstalled version 3.44 VAvmpCompiler, which is absurd."

"Sooooo absurd," Naade said, trying to break the tension. "And you can't bring the super-accelerated tiddlywinks without the double-hydrogenated thingamabobs and can't have the micro-whoozits without the nano-whatzits." He raised a brow, then opened his mouth to say something else, but closed it again when he fell under the cold stares of both Efi and her mother.

"Mama, asking me to stop thinking about robots is like asking me to stop breathing. Would you ask a painter not to paint a beautiful sunset while on vacation? Would you ask a historian not to visit historical sites on vacation? Making robots is not just what I do, it's who I—"

Boom.

A blast from behind Efi sent her to her knees. Concrete dust suddenly filled the room, along with about a dozen different alarms. The floor shook, and it felt like the whole world was coming apart.

CHAPTER 5

It took a moment for her head to stop spinning. Someone was reaching for Efi, her father. She hadn't recognized him with all the white dust on his face.

"Efi!" he said, with an exhale of relief. "Are you hurt?"

"No," she said, but he was already pulling her into the relative safety of an alcove. Mother rushed ahead of him with Naade and Hassana tucked under her arms. Another explosion rocked the concourse. People were running frantically away from the disturbance, some with their phones drawn, thrown up behind them, trying to capture the destruction as they fled. Efi's heart dropped into her stomach. The monotone voices of the OR15s filled the concourse, demanding that the assailant cease and comply.

People were screaming. Crying.

Her mother was cut, a deep slash upon her forearm. But the worst, the absolute worst for Efi was seeing the look in her mother's vacant eyes, like she was miles away. A lifetime away.

She rocked back and forth, squeezing Naade and Hassana so tightly that they struggled to get a glimpse of the scene behind her. Efi worried that her mother's mind was back *there*, during the Omnic Crisis, caught up in the old traumas that lingered at the edges of her memory. In that instant, Efi realized what that conflict had stolen from her mother, and what it had stolen away from tens of millions of people around the world.

The broken bones had healed. The cuts had scabbed over. The worst wounds left by the crisis, however, were the scars that had formed on the inside. Scars that were readily torn apart when the mind wandered back too far. Efi hurt for her mother, and everything she had been bottling up came flooding out of her.

"What's going on? Why is this happening?" Efi cried. Her words tasted of concrete and smoke.

"*Iyawo mi*, look," Efi's father whispered to her mother. He snapped until he brought her out of the deep trance, then she followed his stare across the terminal. A teenager was pinned by a hunk of fallen concrete, out in the open.

The fear on his face made Efi wince. She felt that fear, too, but she couldn't give in to it. She always said she wanted to be a hero. Now was her chance.

"We have to rescue him," Efi said.

"Who's going to rescue us?" said Naade.

Efi pulled out her Junie, but Mother shoved it roughly back into her bag. "No," she ordered. "Let the OR15s handle it. That's their job. Our job is finding a way out of here quickly and quietly."

"But, Mama—I can do something!" she whispered back.

"No, Efi," her mother said again. The shake in her voice made cold shoot through Efi's veins.

While her mother and father scanned the settling dust, Efi turned back to the wall, set the Junie down, opened her tablet, and used the navigation software to guide it into place. The trip was dangerous for a human, but not a robot. She pulled up the video and audio inputs and there, she saw it.

The concourse was littered with chunks of concrete, abandoned luggage strewn all over the place. From the low vantage point of the Junie, the rubble looked like mountains. One of the OR15s guarding the transport cart closed in on someone. A man, Efi could make out through the dust. Very large. Very strong. A cascade of electrical sparks from broken wiring temporarily gave her a good look at his face. Efi sucked in her breath.

No. It can't be.

Doomfist.

Hassana and Naade stared at the screen over her shoulder and let out a collective gasp. Efi zoomed in. She was certain his muscles couldn't possibly be that large, wondering if it was a trick of her camera lens.

"But he's in prison," Hassana said.

"Not anymore," Efi said.

Efi's eyes went right to the gold-plated cybernetic devices

implanted into his fists and spine, linking to the communications piece covering his ears. They'd removed most of his implants immediately after the trial, Efi was sure of that. The world had watched as the court-appointed cybernetic surgeon pulled the imbedded tech from Doomfist's skin, hastily sutured the war criminal up, then sent him off to be locked away for good.

But now Doomfist was back. And the implants were back, and better—not the kind of tech you could get from your local Axiom. He had help, Talon most likely—the terrorist group that masqueraded as a bunch of mercenaries trying to strengthen humanity through conflict. Were there other Talon agents here as well?

Doomfist raised his left hand, and cannons blasted bright yellow bursts from the cybernetic implants, knocking a spatial sensor off the side of the OR15. The robot stumbled in circles, trying to compensate for the sudden change in its sensory input. Finally, it aimed its fusion driver at Doomfist, but it was too easy a target now. Before the robot could fire off a single burst, Doomfist pummeled it with more cannon shots, sending the bot's titanium plating flying in all directions and exposing vulnerable circuitry.

Doomfist laughed, a deep, weighty laugh that Efi could feel inside her own chest. "What doesn't kill you, makes you stronger," he said in Yoruba, leaping forward through the barrage of fire as two more OR15s charged onto the scene. The frayed, rust-red wrappa tied around his waist flapped as he cut through the air. He landed in front of the incapacitated robot and punched right into the open access panel. The sound of crushed circuit boards followed. The angry red lights on the OR15's face plate flickered yellow, then green, then blinked out altogether.

More reinforcements cut through the panicked travelers who were still looking to escape. One robot's arm clipped a woman as she fled, knocking her to her knees. The robot didn't care. Didn't even look back to see the harm it had caused. Talon agents materialized from the shadows, like crabs rising out of the sand. They held the OR15s at bay as Doomfist jumped on top of the transport cart and smashed the glass canister. The robots fired their fusion drivers, hard balls of green light slicing through the air and taking out two agents. They pivoted and shot down two more, synchronized, like they were following the same coding instructions. Just when it looked like the OR15s were gaining the advantage, Doomfist raised the gauntlet into the air, now firmly upon his right arm.

Doomfist flexed his fingers, metal spikes jutting up from the knuckles. He nodded, like he was pleased with the perfect fit. Then he set his eyes on one of the OR15s. He pointed at it, then cocked the gauntlet back. Electricity gathered, blue bolts of lightning feeding into the massive clenched fist. Then it sped forward toward the robot so fast, Efi would have missed it if she'd blinked. A concussive blast traveled a few meters through the air, colliding with the robot and sending it flying back into the wall behind it. Concrete busted all around the OR15, leaving it pressed into the crater. Most of it anyway. Parts of the robot had crumbled away on impact, like it had been held together with an off-brand glue stick.

The impact jostled the broken ceiling, and now Efi could tell Doomfist was close—dangerously close to them. She looked up from the tablet to see a huge chunk of concrete dangling from a length of rebar. Below, the trapped teenager screamed as another round of dust fell on him.

"Don't look," Efi's mother warned her, trying to draw her attention away from the carnage. Efi was terrified, but she couldn't look away if she wanted. Doomfist had been dangerous before, but now he seemed unstoppable. His fighting style was fast, accurate, and powerful, which made it easy to miss how he controlled his body with such grace. The level of concentration Doomfist had was superhuman.

The teenager didn't have long, so Efi scraped together an idea that wouldn't fail. It couldn't fail, because if it did, Efi didn't know if she'd ever recover.

"I'm going in closer. Maybe we can distract him long enough to help that guy get to safety." Efi maneuvered the bot so that it was coming in the opposite angle, away from where they were. Then she pulled up the avatar of the one person she knew Doomfist wouldn't be able to ignore: the Scourge of Numbani, the second Doomfist. The man whom this Doomfist had killed to gain his gauntlet and his title. His hologram rose out of the dust, until it was face-to-face with the successor.

Efi felt the world around her stop. The gunfire ceased, and for a moment, Doomfist looked as if he'd seen a ghost. Her frantic heartbeat was the only sound in her head as she watched her dad rush across the terminal, with Hassana keeping low at his heels. Doomfist reached out his ungauntleted hand to the holo-gram, while her father and best friend silently lifted the block of cement off the teenager's leg, then rushed him back over to the safety of the alcove.

The distraction was just that, though. A distraction. Doomfist realized where the projection was coming from and Efi flinched as he fired a single cannon blast at the Junie. The screen of her tablet flashed bright blue; then the feed went to black. Without the Junie, she didn't have a clean line of sight, but then Doomfist was leaping high into the air, so high he could have slapped the ceiling if he'd wanted to. He came down with the same targeted swiftness and catlike reflexes, but as he did, he drove his fist into the ground.

The impact was so great, it rocked the terminal and caused Efi to bite down on her tongue. She could taste the blood in her mouth. The other OR15s didn't get off so easily. The discharge tore through them, turning metal to shreds. The dangling piece of the ceiling finally crashed down onto the spot where the teen-aged boy had been stuck not a minute earlier. Efi shielded herself as best she could, breathing through her shirt to avoid inhaling concrete dust, holding on to . . . someone. Through all the grit, all the fear, and all the confusion, she couldn't tell if it was her mother or father or a complete stranger. It didn't matter, because that someone was holding tight on to her, too, and she never wanted them to let go.

Finally, the air started to clear, and the sounds of explosions ended. They waited an eternity, wondering if the fighting would return, but all was quiet. Father tried to go out by himself to assess the situation, but Efi refused to let him out of her sight. She refused to let anyone out of her sight, and so they moved all together, slowly, until they saw the destruction.

Efi's teeth pressed together so hard, her jaw ached. Fifteen OR15s lay prone, out of commission. Sparks spit out from their busted chassis. Several were missing heads or limbs. It was a bloodbath . . . or rather, a hydraulic fluid bath. It was pouring out everywhere, pools of it causing a honey-gold sheen on the ground.

An enormous hole gaped in the side of the terminal. Through it, a trail of even more OR15s. What would this mean for Numbani? The most highly advanced security ever commissioned for civilians had been smashed flat by a single man. Now that Doomfist had his gauntlet—a weapon that was rumored to level skyscrapers—the danger seemed insurmountable.

The shock was still thick, but three thoughts made it through Efi's brain:

There would be no trip to Rio.

There would be no Unity Day celebration.

And there would be no peace in Numbani until Doomfist was stopped.

Efi let the warmth of the coffee mug soothe her nerves, staring at the emblem of the Numbani Civic Defense Department on the side. She took small sips, hoping she could blame some of her jitters on the caffeine. It was more milk than coffee, but she'd convinced her parents that if she was old enough to help save a boy from getting smashed by Doomfist, then she was old enough to drink coffee.

Her parents said it was too late in the evening for such a drink and that it would keep her up tonight. After all Efi had been through today, she didn't want to sleep. She wanted to help out however she could.

Her parents stood behind her, her guardians, and not just in the parental sense. She felt like they were supersoldiers, and even the smallest infraction by these officers would bring down their wrath.

"So, Efi," one of the officers said. She was polished yet friendly, and wore zigzag braids ending in a neat bun. She talked directly to Efi, unlike the other officers, who talked around her as if she were a potted cactus. "We understand that you have footage of the attack."

Efi nodded. "Yes, ma." Her finger trembled as it hovered over the file icon on her tablet. She looked up at the officer to confirm that she was ready to receive the file, then she slid her finger in the direction of the officer's tablet. The icon floated through the air, blinked out of existence, before appearing above the officer's screen.

"Have you watched it?" the officer asked.

"I saw it live," Efi whispered. "But I haven't watched it again. Was anybody hurt?"

"Only minor injuries, fortunately. *Un*fortunately, airport security cameras were compromised minutes before the attack.

We're trying to piece together what happened based on cell-phone footage, but so far it's all been bad angles and blurred motion."

"This isn't, ma. The video is solid. 360-degree view. If there is something to be seen, the video captured it."

"Very good," the officer said, then pressed the file icon.

Efi couldn't see the screen as the video played, but the sound was enough to make her go stiff. Mother's hand touched lightly on Efi's shoulder, but it did nothing to calm her. Anger welled up, and all the emotions Efi had kept bottled up threatened to become tears. She willed them away, and only one of them made it down her cheek.

So much screaming.

"*Eish,*" the officer said, cringing.

"It was all my fault," Efi said. "We should have gone to the beach. I shouldn't have applied for that grant. I—"

"Shhhh, honey," her mother said. "This is none of your fault."

"This is exactly the footage we've been looking for," the officer said, "but I'd imagined the OR15s would have put up a better fight. I'm sorry, Efi, but we're going to have to keep this quiet for a while. If people found out how truly useless the OR15s are against Doomfist, all semblance of safety would be lost."

Efi nodded. She didn't want to see those images ever again, and she surely didn't want to make anyone else suffer through them.

"Did you notice anything else before the attack?" the officer asked.

88

Efi almost shook her head, then remembered trying to boot up her laptop for airport security. "I saw a weird wireless signal for a second. '344X-Azúcar.' It could have been the malware they used to crack the camera systems. I . . . can't remember more than that. I'm sorry. I'm so sorry."

"You've done more than enough, Efi. We've taken statements from your friends as well, and they all pointed to how bravely you acted. You're a hero."

Was she a hero? She had given the civic defenders a leg up on capturing Doomfist. She agreed with that, but she didn't agree that she'd done enough. She hadn't done nearly enough.

"What comes next, then? Who will protect us?" Efi asked as the interview concluded.

The officer drew in a breath, then sighed. "*That*, Efi, is the big question."

It was the big question, and Efi couldn't let it go unanswered. The OR15s had proven useless against Doomfist, but they didn't have to be. Suddenly, she had thoughts running around in her head that were too idealistic and too ambitious and too costly.

Well, maybe not *too* costly.

Efi had received the first quarterly installment of her grant money: five million naira, currently sitting in an account at the Numbani Credit Union. And in her Overwatch coin bank, she had at least two hundred thousand naira from birthdays and holidays and perfect report cards, protected by Reinhardt's intimidating rocket hammer. Plus, she expected another three hundred thousand naira once she shipped the next batch of

Junies out. Her profit margins were low so she could keep them affordable to her customers, but every bit would count.

"I'd like an OR15," Efi said to the officer, forcing the words out. Was she really going to do this? "One of the robots that Doomfist destroyed."

The officer smiled warmly. "That's not something we can arrange, I'm afraid. Auditors would be up my . . . in my business. Those things aren't cheap."

"I'll pay," Efi said.

"What?" Efi's parents said simultaneously.

Efi ignored them. "I'll pay. Five and a half million naira."

"Honey, that grant money is for—"

"It's not just the money," another officer cut in, arms crossed over his chest, standing off in a shadowy corner. "That kind of tech is dangerous. It isn't for kids."

Efi looked up at the officer. If she never heard another person in her life dismiss her as a "kid," it would be too soon.

"The grant money is from the Adawe Foundation for me to build robots. I'm working on advanced tech with their guidance. I know I'm young, but I have the experience. I have the ideas. I have the money. All I need is for you to let me have one of those robots so I can build a new and improved OR15. One that can outsmart Doomfist."

The officer with the zigzag braids reached across the table and cupped her hands over Efi's. "Based on what you've shown us, there's no doubt in my mind that you'll someday change the world. We can't sell you an OR15, though. I wish there were something I could do to help you, but my hands are tied."

When the officer pulled back, Efi felt a small piece of paper in her palm. She gripped it tightly so that none of the other officers or the countless cameras trained on her would notice. Efi nodded, and as soon as she was reunited with her friends, she unrolled the paper.

It had nothing but a hastily written address on it:

9127 Alatise Parkway

"Can we go now?" Hassana said. She suddenly looked very young to Efi, tired and draped in an oversized civic defense department sweatshirt. "My head hurts."

"My everything hurts," Naade agreed with a nod. "You okay, Efi?"

She was hurt and tired, but she wasn't ready to go. After a couple quick taps on her tablet, a holograph of a boxy gray building wedged right into the heart of the Arts District materialized in front of them. There wasn't any further information about it. No listed business name. No hours of operation. Efi tilted the screen toward Hassana. "Do you know this building?"

"Huh? Oh, yeah. That's right down the street from my art studio. It's an auction house, I think. Government surplus. Old furniture. Outdated tech. Scrap metal. That sort of thing. You know Sasha Rhymes, the omnic performance artist? She gets a lot of her materials from there."

"Oh," Naade said, pushing his way between Efi and Hassana. "I overheard a couple officers in the break room saying—"

"What were you doing in the break room?" Hassana asked him.

"Taking a break, obviously." Naade said, lifting a defiant brow.

"I'm pretty sure it's for employees only."

Naade tapped his chest, right on the Junior Officer sticker badge they gave out to little kids. "Anyway, the officers were saying they wouldn't be surprised if the whole OR15 program was scrapped after such a poor performance."

For the first time since the attack, the tightness in Efi's chest eased up. She looked down at the scrap of paper the officer had given her and felt like she could breathe again. If all those robots were going to be scrapped and sold off for parts, she would be there, sitting in the front row.

HollaGram

BotBuilder11 is building robots to help people.

FANS 561

HOLOVID TRANSCRIPT

Automatically Generated by TranscriptMinderXL version 5.325

Change of Plans

I know I've made so many posts about looking forward to my trip to Rio to see Lúcio, but it seems like the Numbani Airport is closed due to some sort of major confrontation.

But I've been thinking a lot, and I've got an idea for what I want to do with the grant money. It's big. So big I'm not quite sure if I want to say it out loud yet, but here are a few hints to keep you guessing.

Time to get to work!

REACTIONS

♥ 266   👏 226   📢 232

COMMENTS (16)

BigBadSuperFan Oooh. Bummer. Why doesn't Lúcio come to Numbani more often? Doesn't he know we are his biggest fans?

NaadeForPrez (Comment deleted by Admin)

BotBuilder11 (Admin) Sorry, Naade. We're not supposed to talk about that, remember?

NaadeForPrez My bad. Hopefully there won't be any more "major confrontations" any time soon.

BackwardsSalamander So I'm guessing that's a "no" on the hard-light upgrades? Penelope will be so upset. She kind of scares me when she's in a bad mood. Sometimes I catch her watching me while I'm sleeping. Is this normal or some sort of glitch?

Read more . . .

CHAPTER 6

The auction house smelled of moldy carpet and desperation, like time had long forgotten this place. Just as Naade had commented, the government was trying to quietly off-load the OR15 models to fund their replacements. Efi knew it was shortsighted for them to start from scratch like that. She didn't doubt the next generation of security robots would be more formidable against Doomfist, but it would be a year before all the requisitions and design and red tape were dealt with, leaving Numbani vulnerable for far too long.

"I haven't given up on you," Efi said, looking down at the sketch of the OR15 she planned to rebuild. She wasn't much of an artist, but she was good at making wire frames. She tapped her stylus on the ANIMATE button, and the OR15 galloped across the screen, then aimed its fusion cannon at the wire frame of Doomfist and fired. Doomfist collapsed into a pile of line segments, and the OR15 did a little jig in celebration. The faintest of smiles worked its way onto Efi's face. She'd been experimenting with different personality matrices in the weeks since the airport attack. This one included an empathy module add-on that she'd tinkered with herself.

"Next up," the auctioneer's voice blared through the speakers for the standing room only crowd, "decommissioned OR15s."

Efi's head shot up as she watched an OR15 walk out onto the stage. She'd thought she'd be getting scrap parts, but starting off with a fully functioning robot would knock weeks off her plan. Finally, things were going her way. Cold and intimidating, the OR15 looked so much bigger up close. All bark and no bite apparently, the way Doomfist ripped through them. When the modifications were completed, her robot would look more approachable and be a true citizen of Numbani, ready to defend it in an instant. Efi fidgeted with her bid wand, accidentally hitting the button. A faint holographic halo swirled around her head for a few seconds, then disappeared.

"Careful, dear," her father said. "Let's not get ahead of ourselves. And remember the ground rules . . ."

"No weapons testing inside the house," Efi droned.

Her father's brow dipped low, conveying his disapproval. "I'm serious, Efi. This is an enormous responsibility we are trusting you with."

Efi nodded. "I understand." She switched her wand to her off hand, then counted the rules out on her fingers. "One: Schoolwork is a priority. I can only work on the robot in my free time. Two: The robot must comply with all Numbani codes and specifications. Three: The robot must be under my control at all times.

THE HERO OF NUMBANI

Four: I am responsible for the robot's actions, including paying for any damage it causes. Five: If the robot harms anyone, it will be deactivated." She finished just as the auctioneer was concluding the reading of the robot's specifications.

". . . These models will be auctioned off in lots of ten. Opening the bidding at four million naira."

Lots of ten? All she needed was a single robot. Bids started escalating as Efi's head spun.

"Do I hear five point five?" the auctioneer said.

Efi pressed the button on her bid wand. She had no other choice. It was all the money she had. The auctioneer's slit eyes met hers.

"We've got five point five to the young inventor in the front," he said, his head doing that half-cock gesture that omnics used to indicate amusement. "Do I hear five point six?"

Efi blinked. Had she just been recognized? She wanted to smile back, but then the bid tumbled right past her, rising to six million naira, eight, twelve. Fifteen. Twenty. A steal for that many robots, but that didn't help Efi's financial dilemma. She realized too late that she was a minnow in a pond with sharks: contractors, investors, and government representatives from nations all over Africa and beyond. They wanted these robots as badly as she did.

The next three OR15 lots were auctioned off in much the same manner, but Efi pressed her bid wand button each time, hoping against hope. And then the bidding was over and people were filing out of the room. She was left sitting there, in the front row, itchy finger on the bid wand, hoping for one more chance. This couldn't be it. She pressed the button, once, twice, the halo circling and circling around her head.

"Efi," Father said, his hand pressing against her back. "It's time to go home."

"We can't," she said. "I don't have my robot."

"We knew the bidding would be competitive. We talked about this, remember?"

Efi nodded. She remembered, but she didn't think it would leave her heart feeling so empty.

"Oh," the auctioneer said as he stepped back out onto the stage. "I thought everyone was gone already."

"We were just leaving," Efi's father said with a thin smile.

"No rush," the auctioneer said, extending his hand. Efi shook it. The metal was warm, and buzzed ever so slightly. "You're Efi Oladele, right? The 'Genius Grant' winner? I saw you on the news." And then suddenly, the voice coming from him was hers, playing a clip from her acceptance speech:

I'm so excited to use my creative energy to continue building new robots that can help my community so Numbani can live up to Gabrielle Adawe's vision of being a city of true harmony.

"That's me," Efi said. "And that's why I'm here. Only . . ."

The auctioneer's head slumped forward so that all Efi could see were the three dots on his forehead. "I was rooting so hard for you. It's difficult to watch all those robots get siphoned out of Numbani."

"Do you think any of them might sell me a robot? Just one?"

"Doubtful. They would have bought a hundred more if they could."

Efi wondered if that was the real reason the civic defenders wanted to keep the defeat of the omnics a secret, to drive up the prices they got at auction.

"But . . ." the auctioneer said.

"But?" Efi asked. This didn't sound like one of her mother's "buts." This sounded like one she actually wanted to hear.

"A few of the OR15s were too battered to put up on the auction block. Didn't want to send the wrong impression to our bidders. We were going to sell them as scrap metal." The omnic's head shot up, then looked around. "Come with me."

"Dad, can we go?" Efi asked.

Father looked resigned and shrugged. "Sure."

Efi ran behind the omnic, following on his heels as he took them to a storage room. In the corner, there were several battered OR15s stripped down to their chassis with all of the weaponry removed. If Efi wanted a challenge, that's what she was getting. One of the robots caught her eyes. The missing front legs, the way the arms were broken off . . . Efi was sure that it was the robot Doomfist had slammed into the wall at the airport. She bit her lip. It was in worse shape than the others, but something gripped her as she stared at all that mangled metal. This robot. This was the one she wanted.

The auctioneer nodded, almost like he could read her thoughts. "Of course, I couldn't just *give* the robot to you. An official auction needs to be on the records."

Efi took out her bidding wand, finger at the ready. "You're sure you won't get into trouble?" she asked.

The auctioneer cocked his head again. "Gabrielle Adawe didn't establish Overwatch, then sit back and relax. She kept fighting, kept moving forward as long as there was still breath in her lungs. You are continuing that fight with your work. Numbani can't continue to be a beacon of hope and harmony between humans and omnics without minds like yours. And hearts like yours."

Efi smiled, then realized that the auctioneer hadn't actually answered her question. Or maybe he had in a way. Any trouble he found himself in would pale in comparison to the potential resting within those battered robot parts. Efi would do her best to make this auctioneer proud.

"One busted OR15 chassis, sold as is, no warranties. Opening the bid at one million naira."

Efi pressed the button and the halo twirled around her head. She knew she wouldn't be outbid this time, but she couldn't help but check over her shoulders for competitors, just in case. No one stood in her way.

"Do I hear one point five? Going once. Going twice. Sold, to the brilliant inventor with her heart set on helping Numbani!"

The chassis hung on meat hooks in the middle of Efi's workshop like a side of beef—head tilted, one Branford arm and hind legs dangling, and the rest of the parts lying in a pile on the floor. The robot still needed another functioning Branford arm, a Tobelstien reactor to generate graviton fields, and most importantly, a fusion driver—the only weapon that had a chance at subduing Doomfist. As Efi made mental calculations based on all the work they had in front of them, she was starting to rethink her decision to purchase the most mangled OR15. She'd gotten a good deal on the chassis, though, so she still had enough room in her budget to cobble a robot together.

Naade looked up at the robot and whistled. "Now *this* I would miss a Kam Kalu movie for. Ten Kam Kalu movies," he said, then put his finger to his chin and shook his head. "*Ooooo.* Ten's too many. Make that seven. Okay, seven and a half."

"It's a lot more busted up than I imagined," Hassana said, running her finger along one of the cracks on the robot's torso. A rogue spark struck out at her fingertips, and Hassana jumped back and out of the way.

"She is a bit dented, but all her circuitry is in working order." Efi polished off a soot-covered section of metal with her leather glove. It didn't quite gleam, but it was an improvement.

"She?" Naade said.

"Well, we certainly can't go around calling her 'it,'" Efi said. "She'll have a personality and will be a part of this community. Numbani doesn't need just another security bot. It needs a new hero!"

"Right now, she has the personality of a dumpster," Hassana said, staring into the face of the OR15—a white circle with four yellow lights spaced equally around it. "Just look at her."

"That's where I thought you might shine," Efi said, pulling up some wire-model sketches on her tablet. She showed them to Hassana, who was kind enough not to cringe at the crude attempt at giving the robot a little charm. "The heroes of Overwatch each had their own signature looks. Reinhardt had his mountainous armor. Amari had her overcoat and beret. This robot would have a—"

"Cool mask," Hassana said, brow raised with approval of Efi's sketch. Then she started digging through her book satchel and pulled out a set of colored markers. "I see what you're going for, a little Numbani vibe, but . . ." She stepped up onto the table next to the robot and drew a stern yet friendly face onto the white circle, coloring it orange, with yellow for the brow line, forehead, and nose.

"Hassana!" Efi called. "You're—"

"Making her ten times better. And then if we get rid of these bulky side-a-ma-bobs—"

"Those are her spatial sensors. She *needs* those to get around."

"Okay!" Hassana said. "Well, then maybe we can make them a little less blocky and a lot more stylized. Sloped, like warthog tusks. And we could give the whole chassis a paint job. This bone white and mold green aren't doing anything for me."

Efi got light-headed thinking about all the changes Hassana was making, but she knew they would be worth it in the end.

Numbani deserved the best, and that's what they would give them. "I knew you'd be perfect for this," Efi said. "You're in charge of making her look good, I'll work on finding us a fusion driver, and Naade . . ." Efi tried hard to think of a simple task that Naade couldn't mess up.

"Your safety is my primary concern," came a voice, a high-pitched chitter with an English accent. Efi spun around and saw Naade on her computer, running simulations through the Axiom vocal processor she'd gotten for free at an omnic expo last year. "Yer safety is ma primary concern," a voice said again, this time with a North American cowboy drawl.

"What are you doing, Naade?" Efi asked, then took a deep breath to ease her frustration.

"Helping," he said without looking up.

"Yooit! Your safety is my main thing, bru." South African surfer slang this time. Efi bunched her lips up. Maybe that kind of talk commanded respect and admiration on the beaches of Durban, but Efi doubted the people of Numbani would be impressed. Besides, Efi really wanted to go through the entire sample of voices herself, so she could find the perfect match.

"Why don't you let me work on that," Efi said, nudging Naade out of her seat, "and you can—"

"Find us the fusion driver?" Naade finished. "Because I know a guy who knows a guy."

"Is it Isaac from science lab?" Hassana asked, unimpressed.

". . . Yes, it is, but he was telling me the other day about how he got onto the dark web to get that military-grade barrier. They only deal in MBCs, though, so you'll have to convert your naira."

"MBCs?" Efi asked.

"Modulated Biochemical Currency coins. DNA-coded money. Living cryptocurrency. Also known as bio gold. Wiggle notes. Glam clams. Scritch scratch—"

"Calm down, Naade. We get it," Hassana said.

Efi wasn't ready to dismiss the idea just yet. She'd scoured the net already, looking for a suitable fusion driver, but apparently doing searches for powerful energy weapons gets you put on all sorts of watch lists. After a couple embarrassing conversations with the Numbani government and her parents, Efi got the feeling she needed to take a different route. "You're close with Isaac? Close enough that he'd tell you how to get in contact with the person who sold him the barrier?"

Naade nodded. "Sure. I got everyone to stop saying 'pulled an Isaac.' He owes me big-time."

Efi and Hassana exchanged looks. One of the most epic science lab moments happened right before Naade relinquished his Junie, and Efi had watched it so often, she was having a hard time keeping a straight face right now. He'd ignored the labels on the solutions he was working with and caused a reaction that sent a massive column of neon-pink foam flying all the way up to the ceiling. So now the go-to expression for messing something up with an incredible amount of flair was to "Naade it up."

In any case, somehow, instead of assigning Naade the most benign task that he couldn't mess up, Efi had given him the most critical. "Okay, go talk to Isaac and see what we need to do," she said, trying to mask the concern in her voice.

"On it, boss," Naade said, and soon he was out the door.

A dark van waited for them in the receiving dock behind the Axiom building, way down on the south side of Numbani. Old shipping crates were stacked all around, behind any of which could lie more danger. Efi swallowed the lump in her throat and willed her hands to stop shaking. The van's engine revved once. Efi tried to peer through the deep tint of the windows but couldn't make anything out. The van couldn't possibly be more nondescript. Faded black. No markings. Utterly forgettable. The kind of vehicle you'd want to drive around if you were trading black market goods . . . except this van had old-fashioned wheels instead of lev-rims.

Wheels like those shouted, "too much money and not enough sense," as Efi's grandfather would say. Not necessarily the kind of person you'd want to do business with in a deserted lot. A rotten pit settled into Efi's stomach. Was she really about to do something so reckless? She looked down at the app on her tablet.

Used Fusion Driver, 39% capacity. 64G RTMs.

Price: 3 MBCs, non-negotiable.

No questions asked.

The message had been encrypted five different ways, but Isaac had come through and shown them exactly how to access it. He said it was safe. He said there wasn't anything to worry about, but Efi couldn't shake the thought that they were getting advice from a guy who'd spent half a class period with a barrier stuck around his head.

No. No, this was too risky.

She turned around to signal to her friends that she'd changed her mind. Naade and Hassana looked more than ready to bolt as well, eyes wide and necks swiveling at every stray sound, but behind them, blocking their exit, were two African wild dogs. They were dangerous enough on their own—stockily built and with enough stamina to chase an antelope down to exhaustion—but from their black-and-brown brindle fur erupted cybernetic spinal implants that stretched all the way down their hind legs and gave them even more of an advantage. Efi caught a flicker of neon-green light from behind those mean eyes, and as they focused on her, her mind froze.

"Having second thoughts?" came a smooth voice from the window of the van, now open. A man stepped out of the door and slammed it behind him. He was dressed head to toe in pristine white leather, with a few cybernetic parts of his own, including a green disk at each of his temples. Definitely not who Efi was expecting to get out of that van, but judging from the look on his face, Efi wasn't exactly what he'd been expecting, either. "*You're* BotBuilder11?" he said with a scoff.

Efi nodded. She was too petrified for words to come out right now.

"You're . . . a kid," he said.

"All my life," Efi managed, proud that she kept the tremble out of her voice. Then slowly, she moved her hand into her pocket and pulled out three MBCs. She held her palm up. They squirmed and wriggled, each the size of a sand dollar, and to ensure authenticity, their synthetic blood contained a unique code that couldn't be duplicated. "Can we have the fusion driver now?"

"I've done a lot of questionable things in my life, but I'm not selling an assault weapon to an eight-year-old," he said, shaking his head.

"I'm almost twelve, thank you," Efi said, now indignant. She hadn't come here to get insulted. She'd come to make a deal.

"Well, ten, eleven, twelve, thirteen, I'm not selling! I've got principles, you know. How did you even get that kind of money?"

"I thought you said, 'no questions asked.'" Efi placed a fourth MBC in her palm, and all together, that made up the entirety of the funds she had left. She had a feeling the seller might have reservations about doing business with her, but money talked.

He hemmed and hawed, looking at the squirming coins.

"Okay," he said. "I'll give you the fusion driver, but you can't tell anyone where you got it, yeah?"

Efi put her hand on her hip. "I don't even know who you are!

How am I going to tell someone where I got it from if I don't even *know where I got it from*?"

The guy took the MBCs from her hand then went back to his van. "Wait here," he said.

Efi and her friends exchanged anxious yet excited looks as the seller opened the back doors of his van. He whistled, and his dogs broke into a run, dodging around Efi and her friends with superspeed and precise movements, then jumped into the back of the van. He shut the doors, and a couple seconds later, the van peeled out of the lot along with Efi's only chance at getting the fusion driver.

"I don't sell to kids!" the guy shouted out the window as he turned onto the main road. Then he was gone with her money and Efi had nothing to show for it. That guy had too many morals to sell weapons to kids, but apparently not so many that he wouldn't think twice about scamming them.

Efi screamed at the top of her lungs, yelling for the seller to come back with her money. To come back with her dreams. She almost ran after him, chasing him into traffic, but Hassana grabbed her arm and pulled her back in tight.

"I'm sorry, Efi," she said. "But do you really want him to come back here? He took your money, but we're safe, and you can't put a price on that."

Efi shook her head. She felt numb all over. "We shouldn't have come here."

"Sorry, Efi," Naade mumbled. "Isaac said it was safe. He said we could trust him."

"No, this is my fault. I put you in that position, and now, we've lost everything. What are we going to do? All we've got is a broken robot with no weapons. How's that going to help anybody?"

"Rain on the leopard does not wash off its spots," Naade said. "You're strong, Efi. A little setback like this isn't going to change that."

"You sound like my dad," Efi grunted.

"Getting roughed up by cybernetic dogs in a sketchy parking lot makes you grow up fast. Anyway, I know it could take months, but you've going to turn your vision into a reality."

Months? Efi shook her head. "We can't wait that long. If Doomfist decides to attack, then we'll—"

The forklift at the Axiom loading bay crashed into the building, snagging Efi's attention. The omnic driver didn't look concerned by the incident, just backed the forklift up and crashed it into the wall again.

"What in the world?" Efi said. Another omnic squatted down to pick up a large box marked FRAGILE on the side, held it up high, then dropped it. Even from halfway across the lot, Efi could hear the broken glass shift inside. Then he lifted and dropped the box again. And again. Moments later, Efi could hear screaming—human screaming—coming from inside the building.

"We need to get out of here," Naade said.

"Yeah, let's go," said Hassana.

Efi protested. "Those omnics are malfunctioning. It looks like they're caught in a loop. Someone needs to help them."

"That someone doesn't have to be you, Efi. Let's report it to the civic defense. They'll handle it."

The omnic driving the forklift backed it up for the fourth or fifth time. They were built to be strong, but even titanium wouldn't hold up to that kind of beating forever. Then Efi noticed a movement in the shadows of the loading bay, the vague form of a woman, the magenta cybernetic implants on one side of her head glowing ever so slightly. She threw something outside the bay door, and the next second, she was gone. Efi rubbed her eyes, wondering what she'd just seen, but then remembered that right now, she needed to focus on the omnics.

"They're malfunctioning, it must be an error. I don't think they'd hurt anyone," Efi said to Naade. "They're just scared. I'm going to get a little closer." She pulled out her tablet and searched for open wireless signals. In addition to the normal communications ports that were usually open, the omnics' private ports were also exposed. It was like open access right to their brains, which seemed to cause the lights on their foreheads to fade. Efi gritted her teeth. This was bad. She pried her way deeper until she found the rogue code. It was self-replicating, meaning that it was overwriting the omnics' functions, one by one. If she didn't act soon, the omnics would lose their whole memory. Efi immediately wrote a program of her own, one to slow down the processor speed so she could buy herself some time to think. Then she started on a function to overwrite the rogue code, attacking it like it was attacking the omnics' original programming. At last, the forklift came to a stop, and the omnic sat up alert, head swiveling in confusion. The antidote reversed all the damage it could, and a few seconds later, the exposed ports were locked down again. It passed wirelessly from one omnic to the next, until all of the loading bay workers were back to normal.

Efi scanned the ports one more time, and all looked well, except at the end of the list, she caught a glimpse of another signal: 344X-Azúcar.

It blinked away suddenly, so quickly Efi was unsure if she'd seen it at all. That was the same weird signature she'd caught at the airport, right before the attack. She repeated the port scan. Nothing unusual.

"Huh," Efi said, rubbing her eyes. She was sleep deprived. Frustrated. Angry. Had she imagined it?

"What is it? Did you fix everything?" Naade asked.

"I—I think so. Let's just get back home. I need to sell some things to raise more money," Efi said with a lump in her throat. "Tools, equipment. Spare robot parts."

"Efi, you can't get rid of your tools," Naade said. "They're a part of you!"

They were, Efi thought to herself. *But not anymore.*

On their way home, Efi made the listings for everything she could spare to sell. There was her CraftLife 5000 set—premium power tools she'd gotten last year for her birthday. They were state-of-the-art and included a hard-light screwdriver that could drive a dozen heavy-duty screws into the hardest of metals in four seconds flat. She didn't want to do it, but she had to.

Besides, she'd still have the tool set her oldest cousin Bisi had given to her when she was a kid. Maybe she'd have to manually place screws and nails, but it would work well enough. She just hoped it wouldn't bring up too many bad memories of what her cousin had become after getting tangled up with those awful people.

Three hours later, everything had been claimed. Efi packed up the final box, placed it into the net of a delivery drone, keyed in the address, and watched as the drone lifted off, maneuvering through her open window, then shot up into the sky. Efi's workshop was definitely emptier.

"At least now we have enough room to make a proper bay for the OR15," Efi said, pointing to the corner where her tool kit had once sat. "A place for her to rest and feel at home."

She was trying to look on the bright side, though after the day she'd had, it didn't feel like there were any bright sides left.

HollaGram

HOLOVID TRANSCRIPT
Automatically Generated by TranscriptMinderXL version 5.317

Call to Arms

Well, I guess it's public knowledge now. Doomfist is terrorizing Numbani. I will not stand by while he attacks my home and threatens the unity between humans and omnics. I've got a plan to build a new and better robot to face him, but I need help getting another Branford arm.

I've already spent the genius grant for this quarter and sold off everything I could. If you can spare a little money, please send it my way.

REACTIONS

♥ **601**　👏 **428**　📢 **732**

COMMENTS (199)

ARTIST4Life Done! I can't afford much, but every little bit counts.

BotBuilder11 (Admin) Thank you! We are all in this together.

BackwardsSalamander Ummm . . . so I received a hard-light conversion kit in the mail today. Did you send that, by any chance? Penelope really wants me to install it, but I wanted to check with you first. I would donate, but it appears my credit card has gone missing. Good luck with the arm!

NaadeForPrez Doomfist is going to get what he deserves!

Read more . . .

CHAPTER 7

The donations kept trickling in, and after a couple weeks, Efi had enough money to purchase a Branford arm, refurbished from an actual Branford dealer. It was made for the "Idina" model of OR14 security robots, so it wasn't a complete match, and would require a fair amount of work to iron out the incompatibilities. The arm did come outfitted with a Luxor hardlight caster, capable of generating lassos and energy traps. It wasn't close to being as intimidating as a fusion driver, but at least her robot would have some sort of offensive attack.

Efi needed an adult to complete the purchase, though, and instead of bugging her parents yet again, she recruited her cousin Dayo, who had turned eighteen last month. He was excited to put on a performance for the Branford dealer and demanded to know his character's motivation. Efi mumbled something vague, just wanting to get the purchase out of the way, but Dayo kept pressing. Out of desperation, she told him that his character was a distinguished gentleman looking to add to his menagerie of robots. That was a mistake. Dayo showed up to their meeting spot in front of Kọfị Aromo like he'd stepped off the set of a Flash Brighton movie. He was dressed in a very dapper suit made of silver sequins and a jet-black dress shirt with a teal feather in the lapel. His cane was painted teal to match, with meandering lines of mosaic mirror pieces and silver wire running its entire length.

But it worked, and they got the arm without incident, and Dayo even bargained for white glove delivery to the workshop. Naade was already there, busy smoothing out the robot's metal plating, though to call it a "robot" at this point was quite generous. It was more like a pile of dented and mismatched parts.

"Hey!" Efi said. "We did it!"

"You got the arm?" Naade said, jumping up and running his hand over the box. "Let's open this up and see what it looks like."

"Where's Hassana?" Efi asked, looking around the workshop. Her paint gun was lying on the table next to two shoulder joints the size of helmets. They'd already been given several layers of bronze paint and were awaiting the artistic embellishments Hassana had insisted on.

"Running late, I guess," Naade said before noticing Dayo standing there. He did a double take, then his eyes went wide. "Is that a Flash Brighton cosplay from the Breaking Circuits trilogy? Where Flash Brighton is a human pretending to be an omnic pretending to be a human?"

Dayo dusted his lapel with his knuckles. "Made it myself for OmnicCon last year. Would have won the costuming contest, too, if it hadn't been for that HAL-Fred Glitchbot cosplay, yelling at everyone about mandatory human-hiring quotas. His entire outfit was store-bought." Dayo pursed his lips in distaste.

"No way! Did they see the detail in this stitching? You used his signature gold thread and everything. And your cane . . . is it like in that part in the movie where Flash Brighton walks into that bait shop in the middle of nowhere and is surprised by an ambush of trigger-happy Dagger Sect agents posing as anglers, and he transforms his cane into a submachine gun and turns them all into fish chum?"

Dayo winced. "No. It's just a cane. To help me get around . . ."

"I wouldn't say it's *just* a cane," Efi said, admiring it. Clearly Dayo had put quite a bit of effort into getting it to look like Flash Brighton's. All found objects, she was sure. "It's cool. Like a work of art."

Dayo grinned at her. "Thanks, Efi. Anyway, where do you want this arm?"

Efi pointed to an empty spot on the tarp where the rest of the robot was lying, and Dayo guided the package toward it, puttering along on an antigrav dolly that must have been twenty years old.

"What's this?" he said after he'd parked the dolly, pointing at the cylinder lying on top of a pile of parts that were charred and broken beyond repair. It stood out from the rest of the junk Efi was going to scrap because it looked like it could be functional. The white ends gleamed from a thorough polishing, then tapered down through the middle, a soft, matte black.

Efi shook her head. "It's a supercharger. But I couldn't get it to work properly." It was a sore spot. She'd been excited that it was included with the robot, seeing as all the fun weapons had been stripped away, but after two weeks of tinkering, she'd given up on fixing the supercharger in favor of more important tasks, like figuring out a way to weaponize the hard-light caster since the fusion driver and Tobelstein reactor were both out of reach. At least for now.

Dayo flipped the switch on the supercharger, and a faint beat came from it. The hairs on Efi's neck rose. It was definitely doing *something*, just not enough to be much use to anybody in the throes of battle. Dayo looked over at the parts Hassana had already decorated, then back down at the supercharger. "Do you know what this reminds me of?"

He sat down and wrangled the supercharger into his lap. It was heavier than it looked, but after a minute of trying to get it perfectly adjusted, Dayo started pounding on the upturned end, making up a little beat.

"A gangan drum!" Efi said, noting the hourglass shape. "Like Grandpa's."

Dayo nodded, then pounded out one of the songs their grandpa had taught them. In the next moment, Efi and Naade were both dancing to the rhythm. *Boom. Boom. Pap. Boom. Pap. Pap.*

The makeshift drum spoke its intentions into the air, a call to war, and right now Efi's war involved getting all these parts assembled and in working order. Efi decided right then and

there that her robot should have this drum. Even if it didn't function as a supercharger, it would keep the robot connected to its
West African roots. As she danced around the workshop, Efi
took stock of her parts. They had the chassis. The Branford arm.
The beginnings of a sweet paint job. And maybe most importantly, Efi had settled on a vocal imprint. None of the preinstalled
voices had called to her, so she'd made her own custom one.
She'd taken voice samples from her mother and grandmother,
who shaped Efi's life even before her very first breath; from her
calculus teacher, Ms. Okorie, because even though she could
be a little stern, her voice became so lyrical when moved by
the beautiful complexities of math; and finally from Gabrielle
Adawe herself. There'd been hundreds of hours of her speaking
in the archives at the Numbani Heritage Museum. Efi hoped that
her robot could project even half the poise and confidence that
Adawe did.

"Efi!" came Hassana's voice, shrieking from the hall outside
the workshop. Their impromptu dance party came to an abrupt
halt, and moments later, Hassana stood in the doorway, leaning
on the frame for support. She struggled to catch her breath and
her eyes were as wide as platters.

"Unity Plaza," she rasped. "Omnic street vendors. Gone
haywire."

"They're malfunctioning?" Naade asked, his eyes now as wide
as Hassana's. "Like giving away food for free?"

She shook her head.

Efi carefully escorted her clearly frazzled friend in and sat her on a stool. "Hassana, it's okay. You're safe now. Tell us what happened."

"I was trying to buy us some snacks, but it was weird. The omnic vendors were acting funny. Like you know Ndidi, who has the clothing stand a block from the museum? My mom must have bought a million geles from her, and she even babysat me a couple times when I was little, but when I passed by her, she didn't even acknowledge me. Not a wave or anything. And I don't know, I guess the dots on her forehead seemed duller. Like the omnics at the Axiom loading bays. At first, I didn't think too much of it, but then I noticed all the omnics were oblivious to human customers. Bright and bubbly with other omnics, but everyone else was invisible to them. Anyway, some humans started getting upset they weren't getting service, and a big fight broke out. I ran here as fast as I could."

Naade darted to the windows and opened them. The sounds of the city filtered in. Efi felt the unease and negativity come through on the stiff breeze. They squinted toward Unity Plaza, now swarming with civic defenders, the bright lights of their patrol cars strobing off the buildings and making it look like a party—a party Efi had no interest in attending. Humans were still yelling at omnics, and a few more squabbles broke out. Efi had never seen her city like this.

Ever since the recent assassination of the omnic spiritual leader, Mondatta, fighting had been breaking out between humans and omnics all over the world. Efi didn't think anything could drive a wedge between humans and omnics here in

Numbani, but after Doomfist's attack at the airport, this city of harmony had been feeling off-key.

Efi swallowed. She had tried to distance herself from thinking about the attack. It was too painful. Her parents spent a lot of their time glued to the holovids, watching the news for Doomfist's next attack. They were used to buildings being blown up and neighborhoods being destroyed, but lately, things had been eerily quiet.

What if Doomfist had been silently attacking them all along? Nurturing discord and distrust between humans and omnics, one minor incident at a time?

Unity Plaza was too far to check for wireless signals, but Efi could pull up the incident reports from the Numbani Civic Defense database. She applied a filter, narrowing it down to complaints by humans against omnics and robots, and there were still hundreds over the past week. None of them seemed life threatening, but things were clearly escalating, and it was only a matter of time before someone got hurt.

"We need to get back to work," Efi said, feeling the pressure to complete her robot now more than ever. She needed months, but she knew they didn't have that long. Eventually, Doomfist was going to make his move, and they needed to be ready, especially if civic defense was not.

Over the next few weeks, Efi felt constantly dizzy from the sheer amount of work they had left to do. Either that, or the paint fumes were going to her head. Hassana and Naade were there dutifully by her side, but they seemed less and less enthused. They wanted Numbani to be safe every bit as much as Efi did, but they had trouble keeping up such a grueling pace.

Efi tried to combat the pessimism settling over them with upbeat music and jokes and silly memes she found on Face-Punch. She took a break from coding to slide the latest Marley the Dancing Coconut animation to Hassana's tablet. Efi heard it beep across the workshop, then giggled as Hassana took off her goggles and paint-soaked gloves to answer it. Hassana's eyes lit up, then she exchanged a short laugh with Efi. Efi smiled back, and for a moment, her heart was warmed. But soon after, the moment had passed, and Hassana was back to painting the chassis, and the weight of uncertainty and fear was upon Efi's shoulders again. For the first time in her life, she wasn't sure that she could solve a problem.

"Agba Aja faded out last night," Hassana said flatly. "During the opening for her new collection. She slashed five of her paintings before the guards subdued her. All that beautiful work, ruined."

"Oh, I'm so sorry," Efi said. There were rumors running around school about omnic teachers that had faded out during class. One had stopped lecturing midsentence and walked to the back of the class. He collided with the wall, and kept backing up and attempting to go forward again until there was an omnic-shaped divot in the drywall. Another left through the door and hadn't been heard from again.

Every incident made them want to work harder, but it was more draining than any of them let on. Naade had proved extremely efficient at beating dents out of metal. He was like a metal whisperer, hands running over the rough spots, pounding them with big mallets, then smaller and smaller ones until the metal bent to his liking. Efi wanted to send him the funny message, too, but he was so deep in coddling the robot's hefty right front thigh that she didn't want to disturb him.

So Efi returned to her coding, a cool breeze from the open window nipping at the nape of her neck. It was more than an hour before any of them spoke again.

"Status update," Efi barked out into the room.

"Almost done painting the face and spatial sensors," Hassana replied.

"Just the calves and biceps left to refinish," Naade said, his hands running down the length of the robot's arm, looking for the slightest imperfections.

"Excellent," Efi said. "Let's work a little faster, and we can start assembly in another hour or so."

"What about dinner?" Hassana asked.

Efi grunted, then slid a box of Lúcio-Oh's across the workbench.

"We had cereal for breakfast. And lunch. We need a proper dinner, Efi."

"Doomfist could be planning his next assault *right now*. An hour spent eating is an hour we could spend getting the upper hand on him."

"Yes, but how are we supposed to think straight without food? Without fresh air? Without breaks?"

"Go work closer to a window if you need fresh air," Efi snapped. She didn't mean for it to come out so rude, but her mind kept going back to the way her mother looked that day in the airport, blood mixing with dust as it sped down her arm in rivulets. The shake in her mother's voice as she ordered Efi to stay put while Numbani's greatest protectors were being mangled under Doomfist's unstoppable strength. The memories were warping her thoughts, and it was becoming impossible to ignore. She envied artificial intelligence for that reason.

Hassana was staring at her. Efi bit her lip and apologized before things got out of hand. "Maybe we should take a little break," she said. "We can head to the kitchen and whip up something fast and nutritious. Only, there's one problem . . . we can't let my mother hear us, or she'll have us sitting down to an eight-course meal."

"I'm willing to risk it," Naade said. Hassana agreed. So they tiptoed out of the workshop, down the hall, and into the kitchen.

They carefully pillaged the cabinets and refrigerator for fruit and kola nuts and other easy-to-eat snacks.

"What's this?" Naade asked, pulling a ceramic dish from the refrigerator. He sat the lid on the counter, then took a deep whiff. "Chicken curry?" He made a move to dip his finger in, but Hassana yelled Naade's name before he made contact.

"Shhhh!" Efi said. Then they were all quiet, ears perked like mice awaiting to see if the cat had heard their antics. Thirty seconds passed before they decided they were safe. "Please use a serving spoon and get a bowl for each of us," Efi whispered to her friend.

Naade nodded and scooped three spoonfuls into each bowl, then placed them onto the heating shelf. Efi slid the heat dial right below scalding, and then they watched as the dual lasers crisscrossed over each other like they were competing in the world's fastest game of thumb wars. Seven seconds later, the bowls were ready, a hint of steam coming off the surface.

They sat at the stools around the kitchen island, shoveling spoonfuls of curry into their mouths. The windows were closed, and the air was thick and sweet. In here, Efi felt safe from the outside world. In here, she could almost forget about Doomfist.

"So when the robot is up and running, what should we do first?" Efi said. They may be taking time to eat, but it would have to be a working dinner.

"Well," Hassana said, sucking on a wedge of lime. "If the goal is to integrate her into the community, then we should focus on that first."

"Target practice," Naade said, using a green plantain as a weapon. "Community is great, but she's not going to stop Doomfist with hugs and handshakes."

Efi nodded. "We can't forget training on Numbani's legal codes." Even though the robot would have instant access to every law in Numbani, Efi knew confusion could arise on how to interpret them. She didn't want her robot busting through people's homes because it was the most efficient route. Efi sucked her bottom lip, thinking. "She'll need a little of all of them. Maybe we can take shifts? Hassana can take her out for a few hours into the community. Then Naade can work with her on targeting. And I'll iron out her logical functionality and integrate her with Numbani's law system. We can spread out the work so we can get her trained quickly and no one gets too worn out. Should be fairly straightforward."

"Sounds good to me," Hassana said.

"Can't wait to take those Branford arms for a spin. And we can work on some defense, too. See how strong those shields are." Naade tossed a cashew up and attempted to catch it in his mouth. He missed, and it hit his nose, then tumbled across the countertop. He went to catch it before it hit the floor, but he knocked the lid for the ceramic dish off the counter, and it crashed onto the floor.

Thankfully, it didn't break, but there was no way Mother hadn't heard that.

Efi and her friends scrambled to clean up their mess. Never in Efi's life had she seen dishes get washed so quickly. In thirty seconds flat, the kitchen was as pristine as it had been before they'd entered it.

"Efi?" Mother's voice called out. "Is that you, dear? Can I make you something to eat?"

And Efi and her friends tried to contain their laughter as they sprinted back to the workshop, bellies full and spirits lifted.

They even made time to take a selfie with the pile of robot parts before they assembled them, trying not to worry over all the work they still had in front of them. They would get it done, bit by bit. Efi posted the picture with an update for her subscribers on Hollagram, but as she waited for likes, she saw something else trending. The hair on her arms prickled as the videos came in. Maybe the government had kept everyone from panicking so far, but all of that . . . that was over now.

Efi looked at the amateur video of Doomfist, his massive gauntlet slamming into the side of the statue of Gabrielle Adawe in the middle of Peace Park, turning it into a million shards of bronzed shrapnel. Efi flinched. She'd eaten lunch at the bench that sat right in the statue's shadow dozens of times.

Doomfist emerged from the rubble, the camera focusing tightly on him. He wore a casual agbada, a long and flowing robe nearly down to his ankles, like he was just out on a simple errand to the market. He took a seat on what was left of the base of the statue and dusted a bronze fleck from his shoulder. "Numbani, you see me. Today marks a new day, a new direction for this city." The smooth, deep timbre of his voice commanded attention. He was magnetic. Practiced. His eyes cast just over the horizon, like he could see something coming that Efi could not. "For decades, we have clung to this idea of unity, as if it were the most desirable goal. We humans have opened our hearts to omnics, inviting them into our workplaces, our neighborhoods, our homes. In Numbani, we have bent over backward to make omnics feel equal among us . . . and that kindness is nothing to be ashamed of. I have the same kindness in my own heart. But in that kindness, Numbani has become weak, reliant upon omnics in all facets of our lives. Their power grows as ours recedes. We let this happen, and we do it with smiles on our faces. Numbani has become as complacent as a herd of sheep, out there in the pastures. You frolic together, celebrating and thinking happy sheep thoughts. You are unaware of the dangers, of the wolves that lurk in the adjacent woods, waiting for their opportunity to feast.

"You may think that I am that wolf—" Doomfist paused, knowing that by now, everyone in Numbani was watching and hanging on to his every word. He smiled, then slowly and deliberately rolled up the loose sleeve that hid his gauntlet. It gleamed in the sunlight, as flashy as his smile. Sometimes Efi wondered which was actually more dangerous.

"—I am not," he finally continued. "You see my sharpened teeth, my weapons. You think I am the threat. I am not. I grew up among you sheep. I know our strengths. I cherish our culture, but I also know what you do not know: Unity is a lie. Unity has always been a lie. There are those with power, and it is their duty to rule over those without it. Right now, humans have that power over omnics, but only slightly.

"I know it is difficult to act when everything seems so balanced and just. You could wait ten years, and then realize I was right as another Omnic Crisis arises, but by then, it will be too late for humanity. If you will not open your eyes and see what lies ahead, it is my duty to look for you. And just as sheep must have a shepherd, Numbani must have me."

Efi went cold all over as another breeze blew through the window. She felt the air flow inside her lungs. Felt it meander through her body. She kept breathing, breath after tainted breath. She turned the feed off. Closed the windows.

Doomfist had set his sights on Numbani, but Efi knew he didn't intend to stop there. He would spread fear and discord through the rest of Nigeria, through the rest of Africa, and through the rest of the world. The stakes were higher than Efi dared to admit out loud.

"We've got to get this robot assembled. Tonight," she said, hands on her hips, stance rigid, trying her best to take up space. She conjured up images of Sojourn from her favorite episode of the *Overwatch* cartoons, the one where the captain had so effortlessly led her fighters into a battle with Talon, even though they knew they'd be heavily outnumbered. Sojourn and her crew didn't let up until every single Talon agent was eliminated.

Failure wasn't an option for Sojourn's team, and it wasn't an option for Efi's team either.

"Tonight?" Naade said, glancing at the clock. "But it's nearly eight—"

"Now!" Efi cried out.

"Yes, boss," Naade said, then hastily returned to his station. Efi pushed her friends hard and pushed herself harder. Never letting up, never slacking off. They worked well past midnight. Efi didn't know if she'd ever be able to relax again until her city was safe from Doomfist.

"Faster!" she called out to Naade as he tried to maneuver a leg into its socket.

"Neater! You're spraying it on way too thick!" she screamed at Hassana as green paint from the robot's spatial sensors dripped onto the bronze chest plate. Efi had given the robot two proper eyes, and even they seemed turned down in annoyed slits. Her friends had worked so well together before, but now things were sloppy. Messy. They were having trouble concentrating. "You're doing it all wrong!" Efi finally yelled, snatching the paint gun away from Hassana.

Hassana gave her that look again, but there was no time to worry about hurt feelings. "What are you standing there for? Make yourself useful."

"We're not robots," Hassana said with a huff. "You can't order us around."

"I wish you *were* robots," Efi said. "Robots listen and don't talk back. Don't you realize what we're trying to do? How important this is? You're wasting your time standing there yapping, Hassana. And more importantly, you're wasting mine!"

Efi's head spun at the venom in her words. Where had that come from? But she knew. It was inside her now, the negativity. It was a part of her. She tried to will her mouth to say she was sorry, but her lips just trembled. Her eyes watered. She was afraid. Horribly and terribly afraid, but she couldn't admit that to anyone.

"If that's how you feel, we'll leave you to your bots!" Hassana hissed. She grabbed Naade by the elbow and dragged him away, too. Suddenly, Efi was left alone.

Maybe Doomfist was right about one thing: There was no such thing as unity. She'd have to get this robot up and running all by herself.

HollaGram

HOLOVID TRANSCRIPT
Automatically Generated by TranscriptMinderXL version 5.325

Frustrations . . .

It seems like no one else cares about this city's unity being torn apart by Doomfist, so I'm working on this project by myself now.

But I'm not discouraged.

I'm getting so close.

CHAPTER 8

Despite Efi's best efforts, another month of coding, debugging, and piecing the robot together had passed. A bead of sweat balanced on Efi's nose, threatening to drop upon the OR15's exposed circuits. She gently wiped the sweat away with the back of her glove, then moved her soldering gun to the last loose capacitor on the circuit board. The tip of the gun lit up purple as sparks jumped, heating a tiny pool of solder so she could set the capacitor permanently into place.

"Almost done," Efi said to no one. She was in her workshop, alone. As soon as she shut the access panel on the back of the robot's chassis, that feeling of loneliness began to fade. Efi climbed down from the OR15 and looked at her handiwork. The personality core still needed to be activated, of course, but Efi did a little celebratory dance anyway, proud of how far she'd come from a pile of scrap robot parts.

The robot looked so peaceful and serene, even though she was strong enough to blast her way through meter-thick reinforced cement. The metal gleamed. Efi had polished every bit of it herself, taking special care with OR15's face. Efi bit her lip, trying not to think of the eight coats of paint Hassana had used to give the exact right depth to the robot's expression. And she ignored the perfectly smooth spot on the robot's chest plate that had once been a crater nearly the size of Efi's head until Naade had worked it away.

She sighed, then returned to her computer and swiped her monitor until she accessed the personality core—a combination of open source artificial intelligence algorithms, "borrowed" military subroutines (don't ask), and a few of her own modifications. Her hands trembled with nervousness as she typed in the command to upload the personality core to the OR15.

UPLOADING PERSONALITY CORE

Version 34.5x

Click Yes to Confirm

A big green YES button pulsed on her monitor. Suddenly, the enormity of this project weighed on her. Numbani needed a protector, and badly. There wasn't much room for error. Had she remembered to convert the logic feedback sequences? To calibrate the deep-learning matrices? Yes, and yes. Efi steadied herself. She'd been making robots since she was four years old, and there wasn't a problem she couldn't solve. There was no need for her to feel so nervous. At least, that's what she told herself.

She pressed the YES button. It beeped back at her, a cheerful little tone that indicated the upload process was starting. In twenty minutes, her creation would come to life. Twenty whole minutes. It seemed like that was forever and a day away.

UPLOADING PERSONALITY CORE

Version 34.5x

3% Complete

"Efi, dear?" came a voice. Efi was so lost in thought, she was nearly certain that the robot had spoken to her, but alas, it was her mother, calling from the workshop door. "Efi, we're out of pears. Could you be a dear and fetch some from the grocer?"

"Mama, I'm in the middle of uploading the personality core."

"And I'm in the middle of preparing the dinner that will keep you alive." Mother nodded at the monitor, the progress bar crawling slowly across the screen. "And it looks like you have a while . . ."

"But—"

"Efi Rotìmí Opèyèmi Oluwadaré Gabrielle Oladele—"

Efi stiffened at the use of her whole name, then quickly spit out "Yes, Mummy," before her mother broke out into another lecture about how Efi was a part of the family, and just because she was a genius, it didn't mean she could get away with not doing her share of the chores. That part was true, but that didn't mean Efi couldn't use her genius to get the chores done by other means.

After her mother left, Efi went to her Chore Bot, the one that was responsible for taking out the trash and picking up her socks off the floor. She opened her mouth to command it to fetch the pears from the market, but then remembered she'd borrowed its optical sensor to replace one of the busted ones on the OR15.

"Wonderful!" Efi exclaimed, full of frustration. She still had fifteen minutes, and the grocer wasn't far. If she hurried, she could make it back in time.

Efi rushed to Unity Plaza, taking a series of catwalks most of the way to avoid the traffic in the streets below. Buses made their way through the bustle of rush hour, and above, trams soared along elevated tracks. Usually, she felt Numbani worked like a well-tuned machine—people, technology, and nature existing in harmony—but today, things were different. At first, it was a vague feeling in the pit of her stomach, but when Efi started to cross the street, she heard a blaring horn coming right at her. The man standing behind her yanked her back onto the curb, out of the way of an oncoming tour bus. It sped past her, and Efi caught a glimpse of the omnic driver as the whoosh of air sucked against her skin.

Efi's heart raced. Had she been so distracted that she'd tried to cross at the wrong time? She looked up. The crossing light beamed WALK at her.

"Watch where you're driving, tin can!" the man yelled, shaking his fist at the back of the tour bus.

Efi was disturbed by the slur the man used, but he'd just saved her life, so she mumbled a quick "Thank you," then crossed the street, *carefully*, before ducking into the grocery store.

After taking a few deep breaths, she made her way to the produce section. Efi shoved a dozen pears into a woven bag, then presented them to Mr. Bankolé, the grocer her family had been going to since forever.

"Hello, Efi," Mr. Bankolé said. "How is that robot of yours coming along?"

"Nearly done now, Uncle."

"Good, good." He looked at the pears and raised his bushy brow. "Is your mother making her famous jam?"

"Yes, Uncle," Efi said, her patience starting to thin. It seemed like such a trivial thing. She didn't *have* to be there exactly when the robot came online. The OR15 would wait for her return to receive the first command. And yet, Efi knew she didn't want to miss seeing the robot's first moment of consciousness for the world.

Mr. Bankolé started to count the pears, resting after each number, like he had to gather his thoughts to remember the next.

"One . . ."

"Two . . ."

"Three—"

"Twelve!" Efi shouted, then clapped her hands over her mouth. She hadn't meant it to come out so rudely. "Sorry, Uncle. A dozen. That's how many pears are there. I'm in sort of a hurry." She smiled politely, teetering back and forth on the balls of her feet. "Please put it on my mother's account."

"Twelve pears on your mother's account. Will do, Efi. And bring that robot around when you're done. My back has been slipping up on me lately. I could use some extra help in the stock room."

Efi perked at the idea. It wasn't a glamorous job, but a stock room would be an excellent testing ground for the robot's spatial and dexterity functions. "Sure, Uncle. I'd love to help."

And with that, Efi was running back home. The catwalks were completely crammed with people now, and the streets were no better, but she did know a shortcut. Efi doubled back and took another catwalk, eyes focused on the Bello tower where cousin Dayo lived.

A minute later, she was banging on his door. He liked to listen to his music way too loud, and it was the only way he'd hear her. Finally, he answered.

"Efi?" he said. "Hello! What a surprise."

Before she could properly greet him, she was running straight through his living room. "Good evening, Uncle Dayo!" she shouted behind her, using the title of respect for her older cousin in case her auntie was around listening. She didn't have time to spare for Auntie Yewande's lectures on proper etiquette. "See you, Uncle Dayo!" And then she was out on his back patio.

Beautiful sprays of greenery cascaded over the rails. She hopped over the railing, down to the next patio, and the next. "Sorry!" she said as she landed on a dog's squeaky toy. The dog cocked its head and started panting. Not a lick of fear for strangers. Efi imagined a city where everyone could feel so safe. Her OR15 could give them that. *Would* give them that once more.

She hopped the final railing and was back on the catwalk that led to her home. After a short ride up the elevator, she placed the bag of pears on the kitchen counter, gave her mother a dùbalè—an extra deep curtsy, then ran as fast as she could, back to her workshop. The robot was still slumped forward, eyes dull gray and lifeless. Efi looked at the screen and breathed a sigh of relief.

```
UPLOADING PERSONALITY CORE

Version 34.5x

98% Complete
```

She'd made it. Barely. At least her little errand had made the time pass faster. The progress bar ticked up to 99 percent, and after one final tick, it turned green and played another merry tune.

The OR15 still stood there, slumped over. After a few more seconds, golden light flickered in her eyes, then went dark again. Two more flickers, and they lit up fully. The robot stood up straight, steadied her four legs underneath herself, and raised her arms up to her sides, ready for action.

"New personality module installed. System rebooting. OR15 online," she said. And her voice was like magic, cut from the fabric of the women Efi looked up to the most.

Efi thrust a victorious fist into the air. Her heart was beating so fast, Efi thought it was about to leap out of her chest, and her smile stretched so wide it made her face hurt. She looked up at the robot with a chuckle. "But that name. No, that's no good. Every great hero needs a real name." This robot would be Numbani's protector and savior; she needed a name that would carry with it great weight and honor. "What about . . . Orisa?" Efi said. The thought had come to her as naturally as breathing, named for the spirit gods of her people.

"My name is Orisa," the robot said, settling back onto her haunches and nodding once, as if the name suited her. But in the next instant, she was back on high alert, golden eyes narrowed into slits and trained firmly on Efi. "I will keep you safe. That is my primary function."

Efi itched all over with the desire to take the robot out into the world right this instant and to prove that it would be the perfect hero for Numbani. Her head danced with images of Orisa battling Talon agents and whipping them so badly that they'd never set foot in her city again. She imagined her robot defeating Doomfist once and for all, and how afterward the people would cheer her robot when they saw her on the streets, and maybe they would cheer a little for Efi, too, because, well, why not? They were a team, right? Efi could only spare a moment to bask in these imaginary victories, though, because she knew the real work was just beginning.

First there was testing to do. Efi guided Orisa through a series of logic exercises, and she passed them all beautifully. The dexterity test hadn't gone so well. The robot had been tasked with handling various objects, each more fragile than the last. The first three, Orisa had handled just fine, but the fourth . . .

Efi looked down at the busted glass on the floor and frowned. Maybe she shouldn't have used her mother's favorite vase as a test object. "It's okay, Orisa," Efi said reassuringly. "I'll make a few tweaks to your dexterity matrix, and you'll be better than ever."

"Your efforts are appreciated," Orisa said, giving Efi a small bow. Efi liked the feeling. She hadn't really had the chance to be an elder to anyone yet, but now she had created something—no, someone—truly amazing. She felt all the pride and excitement of a new parent.

Efi reached down to pick up the glass shards, but one of them managed to poke through a thin spot on her gloves. She seethed, watching as blood bloomed through the leather. She took the glove off, then assessed the cut. Not too deep, thankfully. Before Efi could retrieve her first-aid kit, Orisa took the hurt hand in hers. The robot's eyelids twisted, configuring so that the golden light in her eyes was focused into severe slits.

"You are hurt. I am here to help," Orisa declared.

Efi tried to wriggle free from Orisa's grip, but people weren't meant to get free from Orisa's massive fist, unless that's what the robot wanted. "Unhand me, please," Efi said. "I'm fine. It's just a small cut."

"You are injured. It is my duty to assist."

"Okay, okay," Efi said, finally giving in. A little first-aid administration test wasn't a horrible idea. "Let's see what you've got."

Orisa raised her other arm, the one with the hard-light caster, and pointed it at Efi's finger. "I am here to assist. Commencing wound cauterization sequence." A green laser in the center of the device began to light up. Efi could already feel the heat coming off it.

"Wait, what?" Efi screamed. "What are you going to do?"

"The cauterization process is one in which bleeding is stopped by the application of tremendous heat directly to the wound. My programming suggests that you will be more willing to comply if I tell you a reassuring lie to help mask the enormity of the pain from this procedure," Orisa said. She then cocked her head sweetly and looked Efi right in the eyes. "Stay still. This will only hurt a little."

"All I need is a bandage!" Efi said, and she definitely did *not* feel reassured. "Let me go!"

"I cannot. You may be in a delirious state from the injury you have sustained. Please stay still. This is for your own safety."

Efi tried to reason with the robot, appealing to all the protocols she'd built into the personality core, but Orisa would not comply. There was a logic error somewhere in the robot's code, but there was no time for diagnostics. Efi was about to be on the wrong end of a laser that could cut through steel like it was but-ter. Then Efi remembered one special protocol that she had added to the personality core, one the robot couldn't ignore.

Efi shouted out to the voice command on her Junie, "Play 'We Move Together as One' by Lúcio!" Her Junie complied, and her favorite song filled the workshop with a hypnotic beat. Nearly instantly, the rhythm consumed her body, and the fear that had tightened her chest melted away.

It was that good a song.

Orisa felt it, too. Her laser powered down, and her grip on Efi's hand loosened enough that she could slip free. Orisa's head bobbed to the beat, ever so slightly. One of her feet tapped the floor. Moments later, she was dancing. Efi joined her. "Efi Protocol #4: When Lúcio drops a beat, stop whatever you're doing and dance." Before the song ended, she grabbed a ban-dage from the first-aid kit, treated her wound, and then was back at Orisa's side, right as the electronic beats faded into nothingness.

Orisa glanced down at the finger and deemed it properly cared for with a nod of her head. Efi breathed a sigh of relief. She couldn't get upset with Orisa. The robot was only two hours old, after all.

"So, there are a few bugs to work out, but you did great today, Orisa. Tomorrow, we will test your weapons systems." Efi pointed to a life-sized cardboard cutout sitting in the middle of her work-shop. "That's Doomfist. He has destroyed so much of the peace within Numbani. He is our enemy. We must stop him at all costs."

"Your enemy is made from cardboard," Orisa said. "Threat level zero."

"No, this isn't actually him. It's just a representation."

"Your cardboard enemy poses no harm. You are safe."

Efi tried to mentally prepare herself for another frustrating argument with the robot, but looking into Orisa's cross-cut eyes, she saw how hard the robot was trying. It was obvious the robot wanted to please Efi, staying true to both her programming and her creator. Efi patted the robot on the knee and smiled.

"You're right, Orisa," Efi said, leaning up against her new robot. Her new friend. When she'd started this project, Efi had thought she'd be spending most of her time teaching the robot everything she knew, but it looked like Orisa would also be teaching Efi a few things as well . . . namely how to be patient and how to see the world in a brand-new light.

And the funny thing was, standing there next to Orisa, Efi did feel safe.

HollaGram

HOLOVID TRANSCRIPT
Automatically Generated by TranscriptMinderXL version 5.325

Celebrating 1,000 Fans!

Wow! Sometime last night I hit 1,000 fans! Some of you have been supporting me since day one, and I can't wait to show how I've progressed as a roboticist in that time. May I present you with Orisa!

She's amazing. I've uploaded her with a custom personality matrix, and I'll begin testing her around Numbani soon! If you see us about, please come and say hello!

COMMENTS (28)

BackwardsSalamander So awesome, Efi! Penelope wants to congratulate you, too, and all the work you've done for robots. I went ahead and installed the hard-light kit, so now Penelope can better interact with her surroundings. I thought maybe she'd use it to clean up around the house some, but she keeps saying something about an "Error: Cleaning module not found" whenever I suggest it. Any ideas?

BigBadSuperFan Congrats!!! Here's to the next 1,000. Can't wait to see your robot in action!

BolajiOladele55 Your mother and I are so proud of you!

Read more ...

CHAPTER 9

After two days of laying the ground rules, Efi was more than excited to take Orisa's weapons for a test run. She used the term "weapons" loosely. She'd found a way to bypass the field stabilizer on the hard-light caster, so instead of only throwing energy lassos and traps, it could also shoot low-impact projectiles. The lavender-colored light orbs hit with all the punch of a wet, balled-up sock, which meant she wouldn't have to worry about her robot causing any *actual* damage around Numbani. That was a good thing, but it also meant her robot was far from being able to stand up to a serious threat.

Either way, target practice would be beneficial to Orisa, so she and Efi ran to the station to catch a tram to the outskirts of Numbani, where the bright blue sky kissed the golden brown of the savanna grasses as far as the eye could see . . . and you didn't get a public disturbance ticket if you pelted the trees with balls of energy.

"Brilliant style," one of the omnics shouted at Orisa from across the street, a model with a smooth metal head plate with three blue lights. "Did you get that cover sash at Sigma Bot Couture?"

Efi had never seen a robot blush, but Orisa was really trying. Even if Hassana had abandoned their project, Efi had to admit, she'd done her job making Orisa look fashionable.

"Thank you," Orisa said, stopping in her tracks. She looked the omnic up and down. "It appears that your processor is having difficulties in coordinating the color hues of your wardrobe. Do you require assistance in calibrating your visual sensors?"

Efi bit her lip. She was just getting to know Orisa, but it sounded a lot like her robot had told the omnic that his clothes were mismatched.

The omnic turned on his heel and stormed off without another word.

"Did I say something wrong?" Orisa asked.

"Well, you sort of insulted that poor omnic." Efi smiled. "But it's okay. You're still learning. Next time, just say thank you, and compliment something back . . . even if it's a tiny little lie."

"Calibrating empathy module," Orisa said. "I do not wish to offend."

"Come on," Efi said as they continued on their way to the tram stop. "It's important to be polite. People do those kinds of things for each other—holding open a door for an elder to pass through, offering to help an auntie who's carrying a big load. There's help around every corner here. That's one of the things I love most about Numbani."

There were a few dozen people waiting at the stop, mostly

humans, but a good share of omnics, too. Efi walked up to the kiosk and leaned forward for the optical scanner. A green line of light slid down her face, then her profile came up on the holo-screen. She purchased two tickets to Concord Station.

The whistle of the oncoming tram meant they'd soon be on their way. The tram pulled into the station, a bullet-shaped train with five separate cars. Efi stood back as people disembarked onto the platform opposite them, then the doors on their side opened and the passengers filed in. Orisa stood aside and said, "After you," to Efi. Efi smiled and walked into the tram car. She'd started looking for a seat when the horrible sound of metal on metal snatched her attention back to Orisa. Her hind legs were pressing up against the doorframe.

Orisa tried to brute force her way in, and Efi winced as the frame started to bend under the pressure.

"Wait! Stop!" called a human attendant from behind Orisa.

"Stop, Orisa!" Efi commanded, and her robot complied, backing up a meter.

"This robot is not built to specifications," the attendant shouted to Efi. "It cannot board."

"Orisa is very much built to standard specifications. I triple-checked her measurements myself. It is your door that's not up to accessibility standards."

Orisa assessed the door. "Efi is correct. These doors are not up to Numbani code. They are too narrow by six centimeters."

The attendant stood there, looking perplexed at the robot then back at Efi with a sternness sitting on her brow.

"Well?" Efi said. "What are you going to do?"

"We can refund your tickets," the attendant said flatly, with less remorse than a robot with a broken empathy module.

"I don't want a refund. I want to go to Concord Station! *With* my friend here," she added before the attendant got a chance to say something even more insulting. Efi would file a report with Numbani transit, but she didn't want to let someone's oversight ruin her day. "Let's go," Efi said to Orisa. "We'll just walk."

"Efi," Orisa said, once they were back on the street. "Are you in satisfactory condition? Your pulse has increased. Do you need a hug?"

Efi nodded. She did. She was frustrated. She hated seeing Numbani like this. She missed her old city, when if a problem surfaced, someone was always happy to step in and fix it. She didn't like the cold stares. The pointing fingers. The indifference that infected the city as of late.

"Thank you," Efi said as those big, weaponized arms wrapped around her. Orisa cared, even if no one else did. Efi should have felt as fragile as a toothpick within that embrace, but instead, she felt even stronger. "You give good hugs."

"You are welcome, Efi," Orisa said. "Your face is not at all displeasing by human standards. Even when it is leaking."

Efi laughed and wiped away a tear. "Is that your attempt at a compliment?"

"Yes. Was it satisfactory?"

"Yes," Efi said. "It was satisfactory. I feel much better."

Orisa perked, stomping her feet underneath her like an excited pony, and together they walked toward the edge of the city. They'd only gone a few dozen blocks when Efi saw something that rubbed her the wrong way. A row of cars were parked under the pedestrian bridge, caught by harsh noonday shadows. A human stood at one of the cars, a tablet in his hands. Efi could see on the screen that it was cycling through key codes.

"I think that guy is trying to break into that car," Efi whispered.

Orisa looked over and saw him. "Perhaps he has forgotten his key," she said.

"But look how nervous and sweaty he is."

"Perhaps he has recently completed a vigorous workout," Orisa replied. "Like one of those people." She pointed up at the pedestrian bridge. Efi could just make out the heads of joggers bobbing up and down, running between the enormous gazelle statues that stood at each end.

"Maybe . . ." Efi mumbled.

"If he has lost his key, I will act in the Numbani way," Orisa declared, then rushed off before Efi got a chance to stop her. "Greetings! May I provide you with assistance in accessing your vehicle?" she yelled at the man.

He went stiff. "Yes . . ." he said, looking around nervously. "I seem to have locked myself out."

"If you are having trouble with your vehicle's encryption code, I can help," Orisa announced, grabbing the tablet from the man.

She linked with the device in a matter of seconds, then said, "Accessing the central registry: the owner of Vehicle ID 3984HHJ is listed as one R.J. Mohammed." The image of the owner floated a few centimeters off the screen. Orisa looked at the hologram to the man and back. "Facial recognition has failed to unlock your account. I apologize. To access your vehicle, could you please scan your ID here for verification?"

"I . . . forgot it at home?" the guy said. He blinked a few times, then sprinted away.

"He *was* trying to steal that vehicle, Orisa!" Efi called out.

"Shall I pursue?"

Efi knew that she should say no. She knew she should alert the authorities and let them handle it, but here was a real chance to see Orisa in action. "Yes," Efi said. "Stop him. But don't hurt him."

"Affirmative." Orisa raised her Branford arm, the one equipped with the modded hard-light caster, and pelted him with a spray of low-impact projectiles. They were enough to cause him to stumble, but half a step later, he was back up and running again. Orisa started chasing after him, but even at her fastest speed, she was no match. "Halt! Stop right there!" Orisa called. "Cease your resistance."

She threw out a hard-light lasso. Her aim was good, but her anticipation skills were lacking, and she kept hitting where the man was a half second earlier. Orisa did not seem to let that deter her, though. She raised her arm up high and shot her lasso above the pedestrian bridge, looping around the horn of one of the gazelle statues. Efi almost cheered for Orisa's perfect aim, but then she realized exactly what her robot was doing.

"Stop, Orisa!" Efi called. "You're going to hurt someone."

The robot tugged hard against the neon-blue rope. "Negative," Orisa called. "Nonlethal apprehension of the subject is in progress." The statue's enormous horn cracked off and fell fifteen meters, narrowly missing the bridge before colliding with the ground. The tremor shook Efi's insides, and for an instant, she was brought back to the terror of the airport attack. She ducked and covered her head as bits of cement flew off in all directions, smashing windshields and denting the hoods of several parked cars. The blast from the impact also sent the would-be thief careening back toward Orisa.

Orisa snatched him up by the nape of his neck, his toes scrapping against the ground as he still attempted to get away, but there was no getting away now.

"I have successfully apprehended the suspect without bringing him harm," Orisa said to Efi, proud of herself. She trained her stern face on the man. "I told you to stop resisting. The authorities will collect you soon."

Efi stood up and dusted off her iro that looked more cement gray than lime green now. She heard the sirens, too, but she knew they were not coming to arrest this attempted car thief. She frowned at the broken statue above and at the damaged cars below and sighed.

*　　*　　*

Hey. Still interested in taking Orisa out for community training?

Or if you want, you can go over some laws and stuff?

You know more about civics than I do.

You aced every test last year, remember?

Hassana?

Hello?

Efi waited as long as she could, but it didn't look like a response was coming from her friend, so she'd have to complete the community relations portion of Orisa's training by herself. Only thing was, Efi spent so much time in her lab that she didn't exactly have a great idea of what community meant.

Sure, she went to the festivals with her parents, but she spent most of her time shoving puff puffs or shuku shuku or sometimes both into her mouth and licking powdered sugar off her fingers. Efi decided that whatever she and Orisa would do today would be free of expense *and* free of drama. Mr. Bankolé, the grocer, had said that he needed help around the store. She could start there.

Efi and Orisa made their way through the neighborhood, catching stares from every direction. Children's eyes went wide with excitement, though their parents held them back as if Efi were walking a giant, rabid dog. She puffed her chest out, proud of what she'd accomplished and proud of what she was doing. She ignored the harsh whispers and teeth kissing, referring to Orisa as "that pesky robot" and never by her name. Efi also ignored the closed pedestrian bridge in the distance and the work crews in their orange jumpsuits sweeping up debris.

Yesterday hadn't gone exactly to plan, but maybe it was too soon to deal with target practice. In any case, after a lengthy discussion with the civic defense department, Efi made a promise to use the next quarterly installment of her grant money to make a sizable donation to the Numbani Arts Commission to help pay for a new statue.

Today would be a better day.

"Efi!" Mr. Bankolé said. There was a smile on his face, but she could see the hint of fear behind his eyes. "Are you here for more pears?"

"No, Uncle," she said, offering him a little curtsy, and Orisa did the same, though on her four legs, it looked more like an ox taking a bow. "You said you needed help around the store. We've come to volunteer our services. This is Orisa."

Mr. Bankolé squinted at the robot, then shook his head. "Well, you know. Funny thing—my back's feeling all better. I can stock the shelves by myself." He stretched this way and that, a wince on his face and in obvious pain, but trying not to let on. "But maybe try another day. I appreciate the offer."

The rumors of her rogue robot had reached him. That was the

pitfall of living in such a tight-knit community: Everyone knew everyone else's business. "Uncle, I think you are a bit scared of my robot," Efi said.

"'Scared' isn't the word I'd use, oh. 'Terrified' is more like it!"

"You have nothing to be afraid of. I've taken her weapons completely offline for now. Can we at least give you a demonstration? I've fine-tuned her agility and dexterity. She can do anything one of your human workers can do, but faster."

Mr. Bankolé sighed. "Okay, I will let you try." He nodded to a half-completed display of stacked honey bean cans. "Finish stacking and don't let it dent any cans."

"Orisa is a *she*, Uncle," Efi corrected him, "and she will complete this task most easily!"

Efi led Orisa to the pallet and instructed her on what to do. "Be very careful not to let any of the cans get dented," she warned sternly. "If you do a good job, Mr. Bankolé may let us help out all day."

"Confirmed. Commencing tin can stacking sequence," Orisa said. And then she began to move, taking can after can from the pallet and placing them in precise locations on the stack. The first few went slowly, but the robot was able to make adjustments and modifications and became faster and faster at it. Efi saw Mr. Bankolé looking at them from the corner of his eyes. He gave Efi a little smile.

Orisa was doing it!

"They might have a job for you at the Island Port with the way you're stacking those cans," he called over to them. Efi winced. She

THE HERO OF NUMBANI

knew Mr. Bankolé meant well, but Tin Can Island Port was a sore spot for robots and omnics and anyone who called them friends, even this many years removed from the omnic dockworker revolt.

Three minutes later, the tower of cans was complete. It was a work of art. A masterpiece. Right as Efi was about to congratulate the robot, she saw Orisa perk. Her eyes reconfigured into the slit of threat detection. Efi followed her line of sight to a woman pushing a cart toward the tower.

"Threat assessment: Prevent dented cans at all costs." Orisa moved toward the woman and directed her down another aisle. "Threat level zero. Target neutralized."

Efi shuddered. Maybe she had been a little too insistent about not letting the cans get dented.

"Threat level one," Orisa said, looking at a couple of kids bouncing a ball in the aisle. Efi intervened before things got messy.

"Orisa, the assignment is complete. You no longer need to worry about denting cans."

"Confirmed."

Mr. Bankolé examined their work, then smiled again. "Excellent," he said. "If you would like to continue to work today, that would be acceptable. The frozen vegetables section needs restocking, as well as the bread and pastries. And feel free to help customers out as needed, but be friendly."

Efi and Orisa waited for Mr. Bankolé to turn his back and busy himself, and then they did a little dance together. Efi could feel her pride practically dripping out of her ears. "Okay, first the frozen veggies. Just like Mr. Bankolé said."

Orisa took charge, making logical calculations. She down-loaded protocols for optimal shelf placement, and in no time, the store was looking better than it ever had. She queried Mr. Bankolé if she could move the location of the fufu and the amala closer to the prepared soups to ensure more impulse buys. She stacked the yams four high instead of six to make the piles seem more approachable and less crowded. She even alphabetized the bulk nut bins, and rearranged the fruits by color, creating a rainbow display that drew people in. By the afternoon, the place was pristine. Not a scrap of produce on the floor. Not a stray cart to be seen.

"I'd better be careful," Mr. Bankolé said to Orisa. "Keep this up, and you'll soon be coming after my job."

"Negative, I could never replace you, Mr. Bankolé," Orisa said. "My analysis suggests that your many, many years of experience and relationships with the people of this community are one of the driving factors that make this business successful."

"Ah, you are too kind." He smiled again, wider than Efi had ever seen him smile. And there was no longer that fear rimming his eyes. "Thank you, Orisa."

Efi was thrilled to see her plan working. Orisa would only strengthen the community, and she knew how important rela-tionships were. She was already becoming a part of the neighborhood. And Mr. Bankolé was already addressing Orisa directly instead of using Efi as a go-between. Maybe in a few weeks or so, Efi would be able to send Orisa out to tend to the community all by herself!

"You are very welcome, Uncle. I should return to work now." Orisa bowed again, then took off down the aisle. Efi followed, watching as the robot helped a man find the stewed tomatoes. Then she steered a young couple toward the sale on crayfish. Soon, people were directing those who needed assistance to her.

A woman held up her tablet to Orisa. "Could you help me find this?"

Orisa scanned the screen, then nodded. "Yes. And I can see from your list that you are making jollof rice. Is that correct?"

The woman looked quizzically at Orisa, then said, "Yes, that's right."

"According to the most renowned Nigerian chefs, using red palm oil instead of groundnut oil provides a more favorable taste experience. Would you like me to direct you to that instead?"

The woman nodded. "That would be wonderful. Thank you! I'm going to tell all my friends to shop here."

Then Orisa saw a man in a scooter driving down the aisle. He got out of the scooter, struggling to reach a package of dried spaghetti on a high shelf. Orisa intervened. "Do you require assistance, sir?"

"Eh, I've nearly got it," he said, fingers fussing with the edge of the bag. Orisa took the package anyway and set it in his cart basket up front. "Thank you," he said with a strained grin.

"Anything to be of assistance." Orisa bowed again. She began to follow behind the man, ready to pounce on the next opportunity to be useful, but Efi whistled, and Orisa returned.

"Be helpful, but not *too* helpful," Efi said, not sternly, but there was a little harshness in her voice. "Did you hear how he sounded when he said, 'Thank you'?"

"The vocal clips were more abrupt than his previous speech patterns, with a forceful stress placed upon the word 'you.'"

"Uh-huh. That meant he was a little annoyed with you. You asked him if he needed help, and he declined. Next time just wish him a great time shopping here at Bankolé's Grocery."

"I was a nuisance?" Orisa tilted her head in concern.

"No, no. It's not your fault. There are a lot of social conventions for you to learn yet."

"Where can I download them?"

Efi laughed. "You have to learn them, just like everyone else. But don't worry, I'm here to help!"

"I am grateful to you, Efi. You display a great amount of optimism."

Efi tried to hold on to that optimism throughout the rest of the day. The longer they stayed, the more obvious it became that there was so much for Orisa to learn. Her programming was trying to right itself, fluctuating from being too hands-off to too hands-on. Orisa would become more aloof, practically fleeing from shoppers with questions, so as not to annoy anyone else. Then after another lesson from Efi, she reverted to being overly helpful again, chasing people down and offering to push their carts, and redesigning their entire shopping lists.

Orisa scanned the list of a woman who'd stopped to ask

where the ginger ale was. The robot paused for a moment, then she stood back and looked the woman in the eye.

"I can tell by the contents of your list that you are suffering from bowel problems."

The woman shuddered. "What?"

"Your *bowels*," Orisa said, voice raised, as if she was worried she hadn't spoken loud enough the first time. "Your bowels are in severe distress."

"Please stop saying 'bowels,'" the woman said. "And I didn't ask for a commentary on my health concerns. I just need a bottle of ginger ale."

Orisa shook her head. "Agbo Jedi Jedi would be more effective. I will prepare you a list of ingredients. Ginger. Apple vinegar. Lemon . . ."

Efi winced. Her parents had chased her around the house with the Agbo Jedi Jedi bottle on too many occasions, trying to cure her ills. Just the threat of the medicine's foul taste had often miraculously cured Efi of her fevers and upset stomachs.

"You don't know anything about my medical history!" the woman said, her voice raised now as well. "How dare you tell me what medicines I should take."

"You are correct. Virtual Physician protocols installing. Please wait . . ." Orisa got that faraway look, like she did when she was connecting to a server somewhere. "Please provide verbal confirmation to access your medical records and grant me permission to perform a full biometric scan. I am quite certain my previous recommendation for relief of your bowels will hold."

"No, do not come anywhere near me!" the woman screamed, her hands waving in the air. "I want to speak to the manager!"

Less than a minute later, there was a great amount of yelling coming from the direction of the checkout counter, namely the woman saying that she would never, ever shop there again. Efi and Orisa cowered near the dairy products, waiting to be reprimanded by Mr. Bankolé.

"Now would probably be a good opportunity to talk about respecting people's privacy," Efi whispered.

"Efi. Please report to the front checkout counter," came Mr. Bankolé's voice over the loudspeaker. "And bring your robot with you." Efi cringed. Orisa's facemask was made of solid pieces of metal, but Efi could have sworn that the robot was cringing, too.

"His vocal inflections indicate annoyance," Orisa said.

"Good, I'm glad you picked up on that."

"My actions were unsatisfactory?"

"Yes, asking to access that woman's personal information was not the best idea."

"Social etiquette dictates that if a wrong is made, I should attempt to correct it. I have cost Mr. Bankolé a customer. I should acquire him new ones. I have to do what is polite. It is the Numbani way."

Efi blinked. "What?"

"Operation: Acquire new customers, initiated."

"But wait!"

Orisa was off, exiting the store. Through the plate-glass

window, Efi watched as the scene played out like a nightmare, and Efi was so petrified from embarrassment that she couldn't react. The robot was doing her best to convince people on the sidewalk to enter the store, herding them in with outstretched arms and a promise of great deals. Orisa was surprisingly efficient at this as well, and within half a minute, she had six customers cornered over by the produce section. She quickly boxed them in with grocery carts, blocking the exits.

"Do not resist. It is my duty to see to the health and safety of the people of Numbani," she told them. "And it is vital to your health that you consume plenty of fruits and vegetables. Have a great time shopping at Bankolé's Grocery!"

One man tried to make a run for the doors, hurdling over a bin of mangoes. Orisa's eyes turned to slits again, like the threat level had increased, and she bolted after him, knocking over the fufu display and a whole crate of out-of-season cherries that fetched more per kilo than a week's worth of Efi's allowance. The man got free, and Orisa's attention veered toward the other customers. She leaped over the aisles, knocking shelves over, clipping lights. Destroying a bin of egusi seeds. And then everyone was headed for the exits, including Mr. Bankolé, and Efi tried and tried to yell through the commotion to get Orisa's attention, but her attempts were fruitless.

Finally, there was no one left in the store besides Efi, Orisa, and one huge mess.

"The customers are all gone," Orisa said.

Efi sighed. "Yes. Yes, they are."

The robot slumped forward on her haunches, sullen.

"So today didn't go exactly as planned, either, but"—Efi pointed down the aisle—"look. Your bean cans are still stacked. Not one dented."

"The false levity in your voice indicates that you are trying to cheer me up."

"Is it working?"

"I do not think so. My processors are out of sync. They keep replaying the day's events over and over. I don't know where I went wrong. Judging from the tension of his facial muscles and his biometric readings, it seems that I have disappointed Mr. Bankolé. And you."

"You've got empathy," Efi said as she picked a piece of okra up from the floor and dusted it off. "That's a good thing. But we can both mope about it later. Right now, we've got a big mess to clean."

CHAPTER 10

Efi paced back and forth across her workshop under the watchful eye of Orisa. She was mumbling to herself, mostly about how she was never going to be able to afford a miniature Tobelstein reactor. With all the damage Orisa had caused around the city, it'd be another six months before another naira of her grant money could actually be spent on her robot. But despite the setbacks with integrating Orisa in the community, Efi still had faith that her robot could defeat Doomfist and save Numbani. The reactor would allow her to do that, powering her graviton charge to halt enemies.

After calculating how many Junies she'd have to sell to buy her missing part, Efi stared at the result. She ran the calculation again, hoping she'd gotten a decimal out of place when the answer flashed across the screen, but no: 2,749 units. That'd take her months. Maybe a whole year, especially since Hassana and Naade still refused to talk to her.

"All of these community-building exercises are helpful," Efi said to Orisa, "but there's no way we can go up against Doomfist without that reactor."

"Should I research alternatives?" Orisa asked.

"No. Nothing else provides that amount of energy in that compact of a space. The Precision Core reactor is cheaper, but you'd be lugging around a unit the size of a car. The Flexxon Pro Micro T1 is tiny but doesn't have the supply to power your graviton charge for more than a few seconds. We need the miniature Tobelstein reactor. We'll just have to find a way."

"You need more naira to purchase the reactor?" Orisa asked, optimistic and childlike. "Then you should get more naira."

Efi sighed. "I wish it were that easy." She didn't dare do another Hollagram fundraiser. She didn't want to risk losing her followers altogether by asking too much of them, but she did have one option left to make a little money. She had plenty of computing power spread between all her devices. If she lent that processing power to Valor Matrix's distributed computing project, she could make a few thousand naira per night without lifting a finger. It wasn't much, but it'd add up, especially if she ramped up the Junie production as well and asked her parents for an advance on her allowance for the next year. Or two.

Of course, Efi wasn't excited about opening up her computers to an outside entity like that, but they claimed to have tight security, and at this point, she really didn't have much of a choice. She'd grant them access to her computers to crunch their computations while she slept, then in the morning, she'd check her accounts to see how much she'd earned. It'd be worth the risk, because nothing would cost as much as the terror Doomfist continued to inflict upon Numbani.

Efi sat at her computer and created an account with the Valor Matrix project, then set it to work. The program downloaded its first data packet to process, represented on the screen with a square block of pixels. There must have been about a thousand of them, all grayed out. After staring for several minutes, the pixel at the top left corner turned green.

"Well, that's one naira down. Only ten million more to go." Efi tried to keep a chipper attitude, but it was hard. She'd known her computers weren't state-of-the-art, but she hadn't expected the process to go this slowly. "What about instead of watching this run, we get some practice with laws?"

"Accessing the Numbani civic code manual," Orisa said. "Which volume and section number would you like to start with?"

Efi laughed. "We can't study laws cooped up in this workshop! We need to get back out into the city."

Orisa's cross-cut eyes widened into circles, like she was shocked at Efi's suggestion. "I am not certain that would be advisable."

"Still bummed over what happened at the grocer's?" Efi said.

"Bummed?" Orisa asked.

"You know, sad. Sorrowful. Feeling blue inside."

"My insides are primarily titanium gray, but I do feel sadness for the trouble I have caused."

"That's natural. In fact, that's what your empathy module is for! You can process those feelings so that your future interactions in the city will be more positive. You're already learning from your experiences."

Orisa nodded confidently. "I have learned. Even though I am programmed to keep people safe, I should not attempt to access their medical data. And I should not attempt to corral people into grocery stores, even if there is a sale on nutrient-dense foods."

"That's right!" Efi held her hand up, and Orisa gave her a high five. "What do you say, just a quick walk around the block? Let's see what we can see."

Orisa agreed, and soon they were on their way out into the city, Mother's warnings chasing them out the door: "You'd better be careful out there and be back in time for dinner!"

"Yes, Mama!" Efi yelled back. Efi set a timer on her tablet. If she was late to Sunday dinner, she'd fall to her mother's wrath well before she ever got a chance to confront Doomfist.

"Now remember," Efi said, "we're here to be of service to the community, not harass anyone. If we see any code violations, we'll approach people kindly and see how we can assist them. Okay?"

Orisa pranced on her four legs, like a racehorse itching to get out of the gate. "I am ready to assist," she said. She pointed at a maglev car stopped across the street. "There, that omnic is in violation of code 34-342b, driving a vehicle with an expired registration." Orisa dashed out into the road, but Efi yelled at her to stop.

"See, this is why we practice. You have to take the crosswalk," Efi said. "It's dangerous to cross in the middle of the street."

Orisa had a far-off look, her cross-cut eyes narrowed, like she hadn't been paying full attention. Then she nodded and said, "I have violated code 92-574j, pedestrian cross-traffic. I will do better." She looked up at the vehicle with the expired registration, but it was driving away now. "Should I pursue and apprehend?" Orisa asked.

"Definitely not. It is a minor violation, not worth scaring someone over."

Orisa scanned the streets, then pointed at a man the next stoplight down, washing idling cars with a soapy bucket and a very black sponge that might have been yellow at some point. The recipients of the quick washes looked annoyed, but they tossed a couple hundred naira at him anyway. "That person is operating a business, but I do not detect a street-vendor permit signal on display."

"Okay, that's a good one. Perhaps we can help him apply for a permit," Efi suggested.

Orisa went over to the man, but as soon as he saw her eyes trained on him and those powerful legs clomping against the sidewalk at a steady pace, he dropped the bucket and sponge and bolted away.

"That's . . . not the reaction I was hoping for," Efi said. She picked up the bucket and sponge. "Maybe we should adjust your locomotive subroutines so that your walk is a little less intimidating."

A car honked at Efi, and she looked over at it.

"You raising money for something, kid?" the woman asked, elbow hanging out of the window.

Efi looked down at the bucket and sponge. "No, I—"

"Yes, she is," Orisa said, taking the bucket and sponge and beginning to wipe the car down. She was extremely efficient. "Efi is a roboticist," Orisa said to the woman in the car, once she was done washing. "She is raising money to help build robots that can contribute to our community."

The woman nodded. "Yes, I recognize you now. You're that girl who won the 'Genius Grant.'" She swiped her tablet. "Do you take eNaira?"

Efi nodded. "Thank you so much, but we don't have a permit to—"

"According to code 102-542b, children under the age of sixteen are exempt from having to obtain a street-vendor permit," Orisa said. "And yes, we take eNaira."

The woman laughed and swiped her tablet, and moments later, Efi had a very generous twenty thousand naira added to her account. She clapped her hands. "Orisa! This is amazing." She gave her robot a big squeeze. "You are absolutely the best robot ever. Scratch that. You're the best *friend* ever!"

"I would do anything in my power to help you, Efi."

More vehicles stopped to get a wash, and before Efi knew it, they had a sign that said SMART WASHES: SUPPORT YOUR LOCAL ROBOTICIST! and Orisa played Lúcio's "Robot After All" on an endless loop that they danced to between customers. Soon, they had a line wrapped halfway around the block. Then shouting came from the end of the line, and when Efi and Orisa went to check it out, they found that two drivers had pulled in from opposite angles, each trying to be the next in line. One was human and one was omnic, and the shouting through open windows was starting to get ugly, definitely not the kind of language Efi wanted Orisa to be around.

"Sorry, folks, the car wash is over!" Efi yelled. She picked up the bucket, sponge, and sign. She was sopping wet, and her muscles were tired, but thanks to Orisa's awesome promotional skills over the last two hours, they'd managed to raise eight hundred thousand naira. They were almost a tenth of the way to being able to afford a reactor. A few more weekend car washes, and they'd be set!

Orisa turned off her speakers, and the music faded. Then Efi heard a faint beeping noise. She looked down at her timer and saw that it had been going off for the past fifteen minutes. They were going to be late for dinner if they didn't hustle back right now.

"Come on, Orisa, we've got to go!"

They started running back toward their building, but on the way, Orisa pointed at an elder trying to cross in the middle of the busy street.

"May I be of assistance, ma?" Orisa said to the woman.

The woman smiled. "That would be lovely," she said, her voice shaky and her smile sure. She took Orisa's arm, and the robot led her to the crosswalk. Efi felt proud, and even if they were a tiny bit late to dinner, seeing how far Orisa had come was worth it.

"I will get you across the street safely," Orisa said, but instead of waiting for the light to turn, Orisa started walking into oncoming traffic. Two vehicles swerved around her, and a bus ground to a halt as emergency maglev brakes engaged, stopping it just close enough that Orisa could deal a quick elbow jab to the windshield. A fourth vehicle didn't notice Orisa right away and was barreling toward her and the woman. Orisa punched her fist toward it, and the grill crumpled in on itself. Orisa seemed unbothered, as if she'd just squashed a mosquito.

Efi ran behind them, hands pressed to the sides of her head, unable to imagine how much trouble she'd get into for a dangerous incident like this. The passengers in the car were uninjured, but after a stern talking-to, Efi transferred all the money they'd made from the car wash to the driver, in hopes that it would cover the repairs, and perhaps, show her parents that she was at least trying to be responsible for her robot's actions. Efi winced. Her parents. Sunday dinner.

She was definitely more than late now.

HollaGram

BotBuilder11 is building robots to save the world.

FANS **1546**

HOLOVID TRANSCRIPT
Automatically Generated by TranscriptMinderXL version 5.410

Whoops! Still learning.

Yikes! Who knew the laws of Numbani were so complicated? Right-of-ways, zoning regulations, noise ordinances. I'm in a hurry, so can't say much now, only that there are a few more dented cars driving around Numbani.

But, Orisa is learning from her mistakes, and since she's making a whole lot of them, I expect she's going to be a genius soon!

REACTIONS

COMMENTS (76)

BigBadSuperFan It was so good to run into you! I wish that was more figurative than literal, though. Is there anywhere I can file a claim for my cracked windshield? You do have insurance, right?

BackwardsSalamander Okay, not to alarm anyone or anything, but Penelope has locked herself in my bedroom and won't let me in. I think she's building something in there. I'm pretty sure this isn't normal. Do you have a help hotline?

BotBuilder11 (Admin) Whoa, definitely not normal! Sorry, can you keep her in there for a few days while I work something up? Shouldn't take me too long.

Read more . . .

CHAPTER 11

Efi ordered Orisa to her docking bay and told her to stay there until she'd had a good long think about what she'd just done. Then Efi hustled through the hallway to the dining room, running to make up for lost time. She stopped at the door. Her entire family was sitting around the table, dressed in their most vibrantly colored aso ebis and agbadas, like they were on their way to church. Her mother, father, aunts, uncles, and four of her five cousins.

Efi blinked a few times. Had she forgotten about a holiday? She looked down at her filthy, wet clothes, which were more suds than fabric. She panicked. From the bend on her mother's brow, she didn't dare enter the room looking this dirty. From the hungry looks everyone else was giving her, Efi knew she couldn't afford to go change clothes and keep them waiting to eat dinner either. So she ran to the restroom and toweled off as best she could, making herself somewhat presentable. Then Efi returned to the dining room and slid into her chair, trying to make it less awkward than she already felt. Soon all those feelings were gone as she took in the amazing spread of food on the table. Everything looked delicious. Egusi stew? Her favorite! Served with what had to be a metric ton of fufu. And okra stew, too! It was long and draggy, a consistency that took some getting used to, but Efi had finally developed a fondness for it over the past few months. And cherry tarts for dessert? There was enough here to feed their family four times over.

"This looks so wonderful, Mama," Efi said. "Is there a special occasion?"

Mother gave Efi a pained smile. "There is a special reason we have all gathered here today, yes . . ."

But her mother did not finish the sentence. The silence in the room started to stretch thin, and Efi noticed that everyone was staring at her with the same pained look. Then she glanced at the food again. The egusi seeds. The cherries. The okra. The fufu. It was all the food Orisa had ruined at Mr. Bankolé's grocery. He had said not to worry about it, but had Mother paid him off anyway? Efi swallowed the lump in her throat.

"Mama—"

"We love you, Efi. And we think you are brilliant and capable of so many things. But we want you to reconsider what it is you are doing with this robot. It is causing havoc in the streets. It has been a threat to public safety. How long is it until someone is truly hurt by this robot?" Mother said "robot," but it sounded like she wanted to say "monster."

"There are always bugs to work out!" Efi said. "Orisa is still learning!"

Auntie sucked her teeth and shook her head. "And that name! Something so sacred for a bunch of metal scraps!"

Efi cringed. She didn't know how to justify it in words, but in her heart, she knew Orisa was so much more than the metal and wiring that made her. Efi saw a savior, and she knew one day, it would be worth all the heated looks she got when she introduced her robot to the people in her community.

"You are right, Mama," Dayo said, breaking through the awkward silence. "But you should see Efi working away in her workshop—"

Auntie Yewande made a zip sound and raised her hands in a clasp, cutting Dayo off. "Bugs are fine when they mean a half-meter-tall robot bumping into a wall. Bugs are not fine when a two-ton robot puts its fist through the grill of a brand-new Steppe Wanderer!"

"It was a Yoku Voyager!" Efi corrected, the low-end model with lev-rims that barely kept the vehicle from colliding with the street. Efi pressed her hand over her mouth, realizing that her aunt couldn't possibly know about the crosswalk incident yet. She was just stating a hypothetical situation. A very timely, mostly accurate hypothetical situation.

"What's that?" Auntie Yewande asked, in a tone that was both bright and fearsome.

"Nothing, nothing," Efi said quickly as she stuffed some fufu into her mouth.

"We think it would be best if you stop this project," Father said with a sigh. Him too? "We got a call from Compass Point

Insurance yesterday, and they're threatening to cancel our policy if there's one more incident. Of course, it is your choice, and we trust you to make the right decision. But in my opinion, you have already proven your point."

"Yes," Aunt Yewande said. "Why don't you take on a more appropriate hobby instead of making play-play with these robots? Consider drama like Dayo here. He's never gotten his nose into trouble. He has already received acceptances from the University of Lagos *and* the University of Ibadan." Efi's auntie looked so smug in her designer clothes, her buba and iro displaying an intricately laced print and her matching gele tied upon her head in a complex pattern than must have taken half an hour. A dozen of her outfits would probably be enough to buy a Tobelstein reactor outright.

"If Dayo is so perfect, then who do you think it was that helped me get a Branford arm for my robot?" Efi slapped her hand over her mouth again, but it was too late. Suddenly, the tension in the room shifted. Dayo's eyes went wide, and he stared hard at Efi. Everyone else stared hard at him.

"That's *Uncle* Dayo to you," Aunt Yewande said, then she turned to Dayo. "And you, corrupting your little cousin?"

"No, Auntie, it was all my—" Efi started, but her auntie's clamped hand snapped in her direction, and Efi went silent.

"I thought I'd raised you better than this!" Auntie Yewande said to Dayo. "And you would go and drag our name through the mud, just like your brother did!"

"Mama, if you'd only—"

Efi bit her lip so hard, it started to go numb. Auntie Yewande's disappointment in Bisi had been so intense that she hadn't mentioned him once over the past year, and now here she was, comparing him to Dayo. Efi's actions had reopened that partially healed wound running through her family, and there was nothing she could say to smooth this meal over. She'd let down her entire family, but most of all, she'd betrayed her cousin's trust, her only remaining supporter. She held her emotions tight and waited for the storm to pass.

Back in her workshop, Efi had some reckoning to do. She couldn't stop her project. Orisa was too valuable, too necessary for peace. But she did realize that there was a flaw in Orisa's code. The robot simply cared too much. Too much compassion was causing her to make bad decisions. Maybe if Efi turned that part of the robot off, it would help avoid incidents like at the grocer. And the pedestrian bridge. And the crosswalk.

This seemed like a perfectly logical solution, but it left Efi feeling cold. Compassion was something that made Orisa who she was. Did Efi even have the right to decide such a thing?

Efi knew she could be a handful for her parents. What if they had the ability to change her personality based on their whims? If Efi was in a bad mood or had one of her whiny spells, would they erase that part of her just so she'd be more pleasant to have around?

Efi shuddered. It was wrong, turning Orisa's compassion off, but if she didn't, she'd risk having to boot her down forever, and Efi would avoid that at all costs.

With a shaking breath, Efi keyed in the sequence to delete the compassion module.

"This won't hurt a bit," she said to Orisa, then wiped the tears from her eyes.

"Efi, biometrics indicate you are under high levels of stress." She opened her arms wide, ready for an embrace. "Do you need a—"

Efi pressed ENTER. The robot's arms fell to her sides, but otherwise she looked fine. All remaining systems were fully functional.

Deleting the compassion module hadn't hurt the robot in the slightest, but it did hurt Efi.

A lot.

HollaGram

BotBuilder11 is building robots.

FANS **1785**

Saying Good-Bye Is Never Easy

I deactivated a part of Orisa's personality core today. It wasn't easy, but it had to be done. I'm not in the mood to say much in this holovid, so here's clip of some of the fun times we had together.

COMMENTS (335)

BotBuilder11 (Admin) Hey, @BackwardsSalamander, I haven't heard from you in a while. Did the firmware update solve your problems?

BackwardsSalamander Hello to you. This is the human known as BackwardsSalamander. Everything has been resolved satisfactorily. I am definitely not being held hostage by Penelope. If you do not hear from me for a while, do not be concerned. All is normal.

BotBuilder11 (Admin) Glad to hear. And sorry I've been so distracted. Hopefully I'll be back on top of things soon.

NaadeForPrez I know we're not really talking, but this bites, Efi. So sorry.

Read more . . .

CHAPTER 12

Efi's eyes were red and puffy the next morning. She'd cried herself to sleep, but she felt confident in her decision. The project would continue as planned. She stumbled into the workshop, head still fuzzy, and sat down at her computer, eager to see how much her distributed computing app had earned her. Ten thousand naira. It was more than she expected, but not quite enough to make a dent. It was better than nothing, though, so she did a little dance and turned to invite Orisa to celebrate the smallest of victories, but then remembered that the robot's dancing functions had been tied to her empathy module. Efi wondered in what other ways Orisa's interactions would be affected, but she didn't have long to dwell on it. Instead she rubbed her bleary eyes and stared at Orisa's docking bay.

It was empty.

She blinked a couple of times, but it wasn't her morning dreariness and lack of sleep messing with her brain. Orisa was gone.

Efi started wailing. Her parents must have taken her in the

night. They'd said it was Efi's choice! Her decision, and she'd made it. They had no right!

Efi stormed to her parents' room and knocked on the door. "Where did you put my robot!"

She banged for nearly a minute before her father opened the door. "Have you forgotten all your manners?" Father asked, eyes still narrowed from sleep. Or more likely, irritation. "What time is it?"

"Where did you put Orisa?" Efi cried. "You've taken her, and it's not fair!"

"We didn't do anything with your robot," her father said sternly. "We said we trusted you to take care of it, but I am beginning to see that maybe that was a mistake."

"Could Auntie Yewande—"

"Are you accusing your auntie of theft?"

"No, Daddy, I just thought—"

"I'm sure your robot wandered off. You'd better go find her before she causes more damage."

Orisa did have a habit of not listening. Efi nodded, hoping that her father was right. She'd ping Orisa's locator beacon to see exactly where she'd gone. Efi rushed back to her workshop to load the location app, but the notifications on her screen were screeching at her like sky full of angry falcons.

She clicked open the FacePunch app and looked at the live feeds. There was Doomfist, standing upon the roof of the Numbani Heritage Museum. One of the feeds came from an airborne drone, and it circled around him. If it weren't for his massive gauntlet, which was now a matte-charcoal gray, Efi would have thought he was just an ordinary patron dressed to attend one of the museum's fancy galas. He looked sleek in pin-striped pants and a daringly white jacket with a rose tucked in the lapel. The way he looked—the strength of a great warrior and the polish of a cunning leader—gave Efi a moment of pause. He could have so easily been Numbani's protector, but he'd chosen the awful path of Talon.

That false peace ended abruptly when Doomfist leaped from the roof, then drove his fist right into the cement in front of the museum. The grand staircase leading to the front doors buck-led from the impact and the glass doors shattered. Doomfist and his lieutenants entered inside.

The drone swooped down and tried to enter as well, but one of the lieutenants blasted it out of the air with his rocket launcher. The feed went black. There were other feeds, but nothing close enough to see what was going on inside.

Efi's heart pounded in her chest. The contents of the museum were irreplaceable: priceless historical artifacts, the Omnic art exhibit, and a walking tour of Overwatch's presence in Numbani. Losing them would be a tremendous defeat for the city. Efi was so overcome with worry that she nearly forgot to check on Orisa's whereabouts.

She pulled up the location beacon and saw it moving at a clipping pace down Tiawo Boulevard. Efi shook her head when the blue dot took a sharp right onto Heritage Avenue . . . the street that led right to the museum. Efi shook her head. This couldn't be happening. Her insides went cold, imagining what

Doomfist would do to Orisa's titanium, cutting through it like tissue paper as he had to the OR15s back at the airport. Orisa didn't have nearly enough training or the Tobelstein reactor she needed to go up against such an overpowered enemy. She barely even had weapons.

Efi issued a recall notice to her robot, demanding that she stop everything and get somewhere safe. The robot did not comply. A message appeared on Efi's screen:

```
Enemy detected. Straight ahead.


          You'll be destroyed! Please come back.


Combat simulations indicate a high
probability of victory.


        Listen to me, Orisa. You are not ready to
             face Doomfist. Come home. I love you.


Empathy module: Not responding.
```

Then the connection cut out, and the location beacon faded away. Efi kept typing, trying to get through again as tears pooled on her keyboard. Efi's worry and fear turned to betrayal and anger. How could she have programmed such an unruly robot? One who didn't listen and went sneaking out and getting into danger?

She couldn't track Orisa, but she did know where she was going. Efi grabbed her tablet and ran out of her workshop.

"Well? Did you locate her?" her father called, brewing a pot of tea, still half-asleep. It was only a matter of time before he flipped on the morning news and saw the chaos at the museum. Then Efi would be kept on lockdown for sure, and Orisa would be all on her own.

Efi bit her lip. She wouldn't lie to her father, but she could omit the truth.

"Yep!" she said, trying her hardest to sound her usual chipper self.

"Ah, make sure you keep a better eye on her. Who knows what kind of trouble she'll get into next."

"Yes, Father," Efi said, and she closed the door behind her before he asked a question that would be too hard to dodge.

Efi hadn't even gotten a block away from the flat when she saw that traffic was gridlocked. Even the trams hung motionless in the sky. Traffic officers tried to maneuver through the streets on foot. A quick scan on her tablet confirmed that every driverless and omnic-operated vehicle in the area was disabled. It had to be part of Doomfist's strike.

But there was something still moving in the city. High up above, several delivery drones buzzed around, their nets plump with packages. Those nets happened to be large enough to hold an adventuresome almost-twelve-year-old girl if she balled up just right. Efi swallowed. She needed to get to Orisa fast, and this was the only way. If she could get within range of Orisa's local transponder, then maybe she could stop this before anyone got hurt.

Efi typed into her keyboard and poked around on Sky Postal's website. She saw several empty delivery drones in her area, so she put in a request for a Lightning-Priority delivery with a drone equipped to carry a large package, some thirty-eight kilos in weight . . . right about her size. One of the delivery drones descended to her location. Efi winced, then crammed herself into the netting and held on for dear life. This seemed like a capital *B*, capital *I*: *Bad Idea*, but she'd wanted all her life to fly on a plane, right? This was practically just like that, minus the in-flight snacks, the free movies, the air traffic controllers, the seat belts . . .

Numbani grew smaller as she rose higher, and her gut started to slip this way and that as the drone veered toward her destination. She landed at the side entrance to the museum's botanical garden, then snuck inside, pressed through the displays of Numbani's native plants. Her nose itched from the smell of a flowering yellow trumpet, and Efi held back a sneeze, careful not to be heard by the Talon agents lurking about. The walls were lined with masks and pottery and ceremonial swords, displayed carefully under glass and gentle lighting. Efi ducked under the velvet rope of a stanchion, meandering through the life-sized diorama of the signing of the Declaration of Unity that stood on an island in the middle of the room. She brushed past the wax figure of Gabrielle Adawe and chills ran through her. There were DO NOT TOUCH THE DISPLAY signs posted all over the place, but Efi couldn't help but run her fingers through Adawe's signature float-ing above the document in holographic ink.

Then footsteps echoed from the hall. Efi stood still, trying to blend in with the wax figures as a Talon agent cut through the room, gun pointed down, but at the ready. The Talon agent wore the signature red helmet. He was unmistakable. She gulped, and that sneeze she'd held back was suddenly screaming to escape. Efi clenched her eyes tightly and held on with everything she had. Finally, the urge passed, and so did the agent, leaving Efi with a clear shot to the main exhibit hall, where she could hear Doomfist and his lieutenants talking. She crept inside and hid behind a large brass planter, and just a few meters away, Doomfist stared at the holoprojection display of his gauntlet.

"So many inaccuracies." He laughed. "For an institution of learning, you'd think they'd make more of an effort to get the details right. It makes you wonder what else they've gotten wrong, eh? This place is nothing more than a carefully curated propaganda machine." His face bunched up at the colossal ban-ners hanging on the wall. "The Savior. The Scourge. The Successor. Ha! If they paid more attention to what was going on right under their noses, they'd know who was truly their Savior."

"You, boss," said a voice that was all too familiar. Efi squinted through the heavy paint on the lieutenant's face and gulped.

"Bisi," Efi whispered to herself. Dayo's older brother. Her big-gest cousin. She'd known he was hanging out with bad people, but she couldn't imagine how he'd gotten wrapped up in Talon's messes.

Efi turned back when she heard clomping coming from behind her. There she was, Orisa standing firmly in the archway and taking up the bulk of it. She was so close that Efi could have reached out and touched her.

"Orisa!" Efi whispered from her hiding spot. "Please, don't go in there." The robot turned, and it looked like there might be some recognition, some remnants of compassion behind those eyes, but then they became angry slits. Orisa shuffled her rear legs, then charged into the exhibit hall. Seconds later, a firefight erupted between her and Doomfist's lieutenants.

Efi swallowed. Sure, Orisa had her energy shields and was sturdy enough to survive a major assault, but her offensive capabilities were severely limited without the fusion driver and Tobelstein reactor. It would only be a matter of time before Doomfist wore Orisa down.

For now, Orisa was holding her own against Doomfist's lieutenants. She stood her ground as Doomfist raised his fist, the one that had skewered the OR15s at the airport. His gauntlet hummed as it charged up, then Doomfist shot forward, faster than Efi's eyes could track. Orisa aimed her fist at the floor and an orb shot out, forming a barrier of faint blue light. Doomfist collided with it, hard, but it absorbed the shock. Doomfist, however, was not deterred.

"Fire at that shield," he commanded his lieutenants. "Bring it down!"

The lieutenants stepped forward and began to fire. Bullets struck the shield relentlessly, slowly damaging it. Finally, it gave way, leaving Orisa's energy reserves drained, and completely out in the open.

Doomfist smiled.

"I hope that the girl gave you more than a new coat of paint," he said, then raised his fist again.

Orisa slowly lifted her head, her eyes training on him.

Efi hoped that Doomfist would get caught up in one of his self-important monologues so that Orisa would have time to recharge, but he rushed at the robot again without a single word. He leaped into the air this time, then struck the ground with a tremendous punch, sending Orisa flying backward.

She struck a support column, and it cracked under the stress of the impact. Orisa's systems whirred and whined as they shut down. Her auxiliary power light still glowed, meaning she'd just need a minute to reboot. Another hit like that, though, and Efi was sure her robot would be out for good.

Efi ran out of hiding. "Stop!" she yelled at Doomfist, standing between his drawn fist and her robot.

Doomfist looked at Efi and laughed. "Get out of here before you get hurt, child."

"You're ruining everything. Someone's got to stand up to you. And it's me. I'm not afraid. I won't let you destroy my city!"

"Destroy Numbani? Why would I do a thing like that?" Doomfist chuckled, looking thoroughly amused. "Listen, child. I'm no monster. Numbani leads the world in education and commerce. In biometrics. In nanotechnology. This city is primed for greatness. All it needs is a little chaos to bring out its best."

Efi shook her head. "Numbani is great because humans and omnics live in harmony."

Doomfist unclenched his gauntlet, and his posture changed. His shoulders hunched forward slightly, the strained muscles in his neck untensed, and his brow eased. The effect was noticeable—he suddenly looked less threatening, even weighted down as he was by the superweapon on his hand. "True," he said softly. "But this same harmony has allowed the weak to flourish alongside the strong. Imagine how much greater this city could be if we didn't waste our time and resources on those who can't keep up with people like us. I'm a big fan of your work. But I've seen this city, this *world* grow complacent with its technological advances. Only through conflict do we evolve."

He lowered himself so they now stood eye to eye. "But you already know that, don't you, Efi? Or do you prefer BotBuilder11?"

Efi swallowed, caught off guard. Doomfist knew who she was? It didn't matter. She shook the thought off and glared at him. "The only thing I need to know is how to stop you. And Orisa will do that."

Doomfist laughed. "I admire your confidence, however misplaced it may be."

"You wouldn't think so if you knew what my robot is capable of. You broke the OR15s. I made one stronger."

"Yes, but not strong enough," he said. "However, Talon is always in need of new talent. Young talent."

Efi stared at her cousin Bisi, but his expression was distant and cold. It'd been well over a year since she'd last seen him, but still, she hadn't changed that much. He had to recognize her.

Did he not care about her anymore? Not even a little? Or was he too ashamed of the company he was now keeping?

Efi growled at Doomfist for the role he'd played in taking Bisi away from her and her family. "Talon is trying to tear us apart, but together, the citizens of Numbani are already much stronger than you will ever be."

Doomfist frowned and raised his hand cannon. He pointed it at Orisa, but Efi moved to stand in front of her.

"You'll have to shoot me, too," Efi said. "You say you're not a monster. Prove it! Take your lieutenants and leave this place."

"You don't want to get in the way of this." Doomfist pointed his hand cannon right at Efi. He jumped into the air, ready to attack, but at the last possible moment, Efi heard her robot coming back online.

Orisa was still crumpled up in a heap but managed to fire a large green orb into the room, and one by one Doomfist's lieutenants were dragged toward it. A graviton pulse? But how? Orisa didn't have that capability yet. The lieutenants hit the wall with such a force that they were knocked out cold. Doomfist just barely escaped the pull of the pulse and aimed at Orisa again. All hints of kindness had disappeared from his face. Now there was only fury.

Orisa threw up her shield again, this time with Efi tucked safely behind it.

The shield held as Doomfist slammed it with bullets. Efi felt a surge of heat coming off the shield, like she was standing too close to an oven, but nothing more. More blasts came, but she became more confident that the barrier would hold, at least long enough for her to summon some backup. Efi worked her way through the code Doomfist had used to deactivate the vehicles within Numbani. Finally, as the congestion eased, she heard sirens wailing in the distance, getting closer. Her code had disseminated. Help was on the way and Orisa's graviton pulse was almost recharged. Orisa didn't have a whole lot left in her, but it would be enough to see that justice was served.

Doomfist stopped firing, then called his lieutenants to regroup. At least the ones that were still capable of walking.

He looked back at Efi before leaving. "You should learn your history, girl, because I promise you, it's about to repeat itself." And then he and his crew were gone, including Bisi—exiting through the same massive chasm they'd punched into the museum. She couldn't believe her cousin was involved with Talon. Somehow, that cut more deeply than any of the nonsense Doomfist had said to her.

Efi took a deep breath, then looked Orisa up and down, assessing the damage. Her robot was already in the middle of running a self-diagnostic, and it seemed like nearly every system had been compromised in some way. Efi willed the tears away and focused on being a roboticist, looking at a machine that needed to be repaired rather than seeing a severely wounded friend. Both front legs were nonfunctional, and her chest plate had cracked. Still, Orisa had stood up to him better than any of the OR15s at the airport had. This was merely a setback. She would rebuild her robot yet again, stronger, faster, better.

"What is this?" Efi asked, pointing to the device mounted on

Orisa's arm. It was cobbled together from mismatched parts, a patchwork of metal and wires. Then she saw the Junkertown graffiti on the side. Efi grimaced. It was made by the community of misfits living down in what was left of Australia after they'd blown up the fusion core on an omnium plant.

"A graviton reactor," Orisa said, her voice slow and warbling. "It was necessary to gain a tactical advantage."

"Yes, but that's for me to worry about, not you. This is Junker tech. It's probably irradiated and just as likely to blow up in your face as it is to work. We're going to have to send that back as soon as we get you home. And why did you cut off your remote interface like that? You disobeyed my commands."

"Doomfist is the enemy. You said we must stop him at all costs."

"Yes, well, maybe that was a bad choice of words. There are other factors you need to figure in. Besides, we need to finish your training first, and . . . and where did you even get the money to buy a reactor?"

"I used my processors to run your distributed computing app. It was the most logical and efficient solution to raise funds for the reactor."

"Your processors?" Efi said. She'd steeled her nerves enough to stand up to Doomfist, but now she could barely keep her feet beneath her. "Is that why you've been distracted? You've put yourself in danger. You've broken half the city. You've caused more damage than Doomfist!" Efi bit her lip. She shouldn't have said that last part, but she wanted Orisa to understand that what she did was wrong, so she wouldn't hurt herself like this again. "You can't go running around the city without concern for your safety. Do you know how worried I was when you weren't in your docking bay? Next time, if there is a next time, I swear I'm going to—"

Efi stopped herself and swallowed. She looked around the museum, noting cracks and scorch marks on the floor, bullet holes peppering the walls. Any one of those threats could have torn Efi apart. She'd defied her parents and had put herself in danger. She couldn't even imagine how frightened they were for her right now. Efi called them right away, but instead of yelling at her, they were crying, and her mother was getting tears all over the screen. She told Efi to get to a hiding spot and stay there, and that they would be on their way.

As soon as Efi disconnected, she did exactly what her parents had told her. Doomfist had gotten the best of them, but at least the important pieces of their heritage had been saved. And as Efi hid among Numbani's precious treasures, she couldn't help but wonder what Doomfist meant about history repeating itself. What was he after?

Chaos. He wanted chaos. And what better way to sow chaos than to give Numbani its own personal Omnic Crisis? Doomfist was trying to drive a wedge between humans and omnics, igniting distrust through the series of small malfunctions that would snowball into something much more significant. And now that Efi knew what Doomfist was up to, she had to put a stop to it.

The minutes passed like hours, but soon the whole museum was buzzing with civic defenders, and with reporters swarming around the parmiter like vultures, looking to be the first to get a comment directly from Efi. Finally, Efi's parents arrived, and were ushered to meet her in the quiet of one of the interior rooms. Efi cringed as her father opened his mouth to reprimand her, but one of the reporters swooped in, just in time.

She flashed a green holographic press badge, which lingered in the air a few moments before it fizzled into nothingness. "Bethany Steele with *Atlas News*," the omnic reporter said, addressing Mother and Father. Efi's eyebrows crawled up her forehead. She thought she'd just be on the local stations. This was international! "You must be the proud parents of this young Numbani hero."

"I—um—" Father fumbled for words. Efi had never seen him falter like this. He was used to giving lectures in front of hundreds of people. "Yes. Yes, we are."

"I know Gabrielle Adawe would be proud as well," the reporter said. "All of Numbani has just witnessed your daughter in action, saving some of the city's most priceless artifacts. May we have a few words with Efi?"

Mother looked around, realizing a crowd had followed them in, and she becamed starry-eyed from all the attention. "From the day our daughter was born, she meant the world to us," Mother said, patting her gele into the perfect position on top of her head and adjusting herself so that she was square in the reporter's camera. "It is our pleasure to share her brilliance with the world . . ."

Her mother continued to regale the entire planet with Efi's acheivements, and by the transitive property, her parents' achievements. Efi sighed with relief. It looked like with this sudden fame, she'd avoid her parents' wrath. At least for a while.

HollaGram

HOLOVID TRANSCRIPT
Automatically Generated by TranscriptMinderXL version 5.410

I'm on the News!

Today was INTENSE! But I ended up on the news. Check out this clip:

"I wasn't afraid of Doomfist, because I was done being afraid. Fear is what he wants, and I didn't give it to him. He can destroy our buildings. Mess up our traffic. But he can't take away what makes us citizens of Numbani. He can't take away our unity unless we let him. And I won't let him.

"Unity Day was canceled because of his attack on our city, but we can't let another month go by without it. We will reclaim our Unity. Now."

REACTIONS

 1253 👏 301 📢 231

COMMENTS (335)

Dayo @BotBuilder11 We should do the Unity Play, even if it's super late. What do you think?

BotBuilder11 (Admin) Great Idea! And we can sell tickets to raise money for the victims of all the Talon attacks!

Lúcio (verified) You make the world great, Efi. You gotta believe!

BotBuilder11 (Admin) Hyperventilating now. BRB.

Dayo Efi!

BotBuilder11 (Admin) I know!!!

Read more . . .

CHAPTER 13

Efi still couldn't believe that Lúcio—THE LÚCIO—had commented on her holovid. Her feet hadn't touched the ground for the entire day. She'd printed the comment thread out, gotten it framed, and now it sat next to her bed. She also had one laminated to keep in her satchel. And while she was at it, she had it put onto a custom bowl for her Lúcio-Oh's, but the custom order wouldn't be here for days.

As happy as she was, she still couldn't shake the feeling of shock from seeing her cousin Bisi working with Doomfist. How had someone with so much potential, so bright of a future, made such an awful choice? Could she have done anything to stop him from making it? Efi needed someone to talk to so she could process these feelings—how her day had contained both an epic high and a critical low, but the two friends she was closest to . . . the only ones who'd understand what she was going through . . . she'd pushed them away.

Efi thought about what Orisa had said at the grocer's, that if you hurt someone, you should make it up to them. Efi knew that she'd hurt her friends. In the moment, she'd thought everything she said was justified, but now she saw that what she'd done was ugly and wrong. It was time to make it up to them.

At school the next day, Efi had a plan. However, when she entered the building, the plan was toast. Everywhere she went, she was swamped by students, asking her about going up against Doomfist, asking about the robot. Some even asked her for her autograph, like she was a star! Efi felt herself swelling with pride after all the doubt people had initially shown toward Orisa, but she was also nervous . . . Orisa still had problems that needed working out. She dodged people's questions as she tried to weave her way over to her friends, but she couldn't get close enough to Hassana and Naade to apologize. They'd see her coming, followed by a mob of fans, and they'd disappear down the hall.

When the bell rang for lunch, Efi held her tablet up to her face for a disguise and made a run for the library, lying low until everyone had started eating. It was stewed beans day, so eyes were mostly cast down, focused intently on shoving big spoonfuls of it into their mouths.

Efi sat down at the lunch table across from Naade and Hassana.

"I come bearing apology presents," she said, setting an extra helping of stewed beans on Naade's plate, and a fruit cup on Hassana's. "I'm sorry I got so caught up in this project. I was stressed, but I never should have taken it out on you."

Naade looked up at her, tentatively, through his lashes, but Hassana could hold a grudge with the best of them.

"You're—" Naade winced, then looked back down at his tray, probably after taking a kick to the shin. "She said she was sorry," he whispered at Hassana out the side of his mouth.

"If she was *really* sorry," Hassana said, looking directly at Naade and pretending that Efi didn't exist, "she would have mentioned our names on the news. She's been on a few times now! Everyone's going on about how she's such a genius, and how she's so brave, but we've been there by her side since day one. We were there at the airport. She needs us to do her dirty work for her, but as soon as it's time to take credit, she's up front and center. Every time!"

Efi gasped and sat back. Hassana's words were sharp, but true. She hadn't been exactly thoughtful in her opportunities to publicly acknowledge her friends, and a fruit cup wasn't about to rectify that. Well, Efi couldn't make a public statement on the news right now, but she could see to it that her friends got the recognition they deserved.

Efi climbed up onto the lunch table. "Attention, everyone. I would like to acknowledge the contributions of my two best friends, Hassana and Naade, in their efforts to build Orisa, the robot who scared off Doomfist."

Hassana looked up at Efi, embarrassed. "Get down from there. The principal is coming!"

Efi glanced toward the administrative offices and saw Mr. Egwe walking toward them, his heavy metal footsteps clanking against the linoleum floor. Efi knew he did so on purpose, because he had been originally designed as a librarian, and his functionality took into account the need for quiet and discreetness. He meant to be loud and intimidating, but Efi didn't dare budge from her perch overlooking the entire cafeteria.

"You congratulate me in the halls," she shouted, "and I'm excited to talk to each and every one of you, but also thank my two best friends when you see them. Because they are as big a part of this as I am."

"Ms. Oladele," the principal said. "Please come down from there, or you will have to face disciplinary actions."

Efi stood still, her pristine academic career flashing before her eyes. But, no, this was just as important. Her friends had stood faithfully by her, and now it was her turn to do the same.

She continued. "Hassana is the creative mind behind Orisa's new look. Everything that's beautiful and graceful about that robot is due to her keen vision. She made Orisa a work of art. And Naade . . . you all should have seen the shape the OR15 chassis was in when it came to us. Busted and dented, nearly beyond recognition. Naade sculpted every piece of that metal until it was strong and sure. Without him, Orisa would have crumbled in battle. They are both heroes as well and should be celebrated as such."

"Ms. Oladele," the principal said, again, though this time the urgency was more pronounced. "Please, step down from there and come to my office."

Efi had been to the principal's office many times: when she'd received the Gallant Minds Award, for twenty consecutive honor rolls, for every science fair trophy presentation except for the one with the graviton incident. She knew the principal very well. This scowl along his brow was new, though—metal appendages jutting out from the chrome of his domed head. It was a prudent feature for an omnic principal, and it was very effective on Efi. She stepped down from the table, but the entire cafeteria started chanting all three of their names. Efi. Hassana. Naade.

Efi smiled to herself, even though she knew her day was only going to get worse.

"Detention!" Efi's mother said, looking at her daughter like she was an alien. "Detention!"

It was the only word she'd said to Efi since she'd gotten home. Efi had never seen her mother this disappointed. Even after sneaking out of the house to go fight against bad guys, Efi hadn't had this much of a guilt trip dropped on her. She was in trouble this time. *Major trouble.* Mother had a way with words, stressing different syllables with each repetition, so that Efi had to read between the lines to catch her meaning.

"Detention." *My daughter was acting up in front of the principal, after all these years of raising her to respect her elders and her community.*

"But Mama, I—"

"Detention?" *Couldn't you have waited until after school? You've ruined your perfect record.*

"I had to, Mama, because—"

"Detention!" *There are repercussions for your actions.*

Efi knew she had to think of something to pacify her mother. She started throwing out self-punishments. "I'll clean my room. I'll clean the whole house! I'll have everything spotless."

Mother shook her head sullenly. "Detention . . ."

That wasn't cutting it. Efi upped the ante. "I'll stop posting holovids for a week, a month. However long it takes to earn your trust back."

Mother sighed. "Detention. Detention."

Better, Efi thought. Mother seemed a little less bothered. Efi needed a big sacrifice, and she knew just the one to make. "No workshop for a week. No robots, either. I'll . . . just interact with people. Dayo and I are going to be working on the fundraiser play anyway. I'll be spending my time with his drama club. I'll be out of the house, making new friends—"

"Efi," her mother said. Finally! Actual words. "You better shine your eyes, my friend. I didn't give birth to you just so you can kill me with worry. You need to start taking your actions seriously. I don't know what's gotten into you lately."

Her mother sat down beside Efi on the bed. "Your father and I, we always expect some level of chaos from your inventions. It comes with having a daughter who's a genius. But this robot has gotten you deeper and deeper into trouble."

"Mama, I—"

"I'm not talking about the produce or the bridge or the other chaos you've caused, Efi. That robot led you into a confrontation with a *terrorist*. You could have died. We could have lost you.

You're an extraordinary person, but all this is starting to feel too big for one child."

Efi bit her lip. She hated that word, but her mother was right and Efi knew it. She shouldn't have followed Orisa to the museum, but it was like she couldn't stop. Her body was moving before her mind connected with the logical functions of her brain. It was only after the confrontation had ended that she realized what she'd done. But even then she couldn't bring herself to fully repent. Numbani needed a hero, and Orisa was becoming that. She was becoming hope for the people of Numbani to unite and fight back against Doomfist.

"You know how your father and I feel about Orisa. And you know what we discussed after the museum—she needs to stay out of danger." Her mother's face trembled for a moment as she took Efi's hand. "*You* need to stay out of danger. No more second chances. Promise me you'll think before you act next time."

"I promise, Mummy."

Her mother sighed once more for good measure, then left Efi alone in her room. "Detention, detention," Efi heard her mother mumbling down the hall. As soon as the coast was clear, she messaged Hassana.

Are we okay?

Yeah. Is your mom mad?

Very. But it was worth it.

Efi had her friends back, but now she'd put Orisa in exile, and it wasn't fair to the robot. She asked Hassana and Naade if they'd be willing to stop by the workshop to finish up the last of the repairs, and after that, if they could train Orisa while Efi prepped for the play. Naade could help out, too, with tactical improvements, even if all of this combat expertise came from watching action movies and playing video games.

A week would go by quickly. Or at least, that's what Efi hoped.

HollaGram

REACTIONS

 ♥ 4 👏 1 📣 0

COMMENTS (5)

NaadeForPrez Efi? Are you okay?

BotBuilder11 (Admin) ER.kokwpwjem099 This 5 second trick can prevent debt collectors from seizing your assets!!! Click HERE to see!

NaadeForPrez I think you might be hacked.

Read more ...

CHAPTER 14

Excited chattering filled the theater, accompanied by the smacking of wood and the clattering of metal. The set for the Unity Day play was being brought out of storage and reassembled. As soon as Efi walked in, she noticed the big frown on Joké's face as she looked down at her tablet, and then back up at the stage. The props they'd spent so much time putting together were finally going to be used after all, but whoever had stored them hadn't been very careful, and they were dinged up and scuffed.

Efi guessed that the downside of using junk to build props was that the junk seemed desperate to return to its previous state.

"Hey, Sam. Let's get the skyline repainted. Dayo, check the lighting to see if any bulbs are damaged." Joké looked back at Efi. "Oh, hey! Are you here to help out?"

"Definitely," Efi said. "What do you want me to do?"

"Hmmm. How about ironing out the folds in the costumes?"

Joké asked. "I wish we had something better to offer. I've tried to assign this job to three people now, and every time, they come back a few minutes later saying that something important has come up and they can't do it."

Efi grinned. "I'm happy to be involved in the play however I can. If ironing is what you need, you're going to have the most unwrinkled costumes this theater has ever seen!"

"Whoa. Love the enthusiasm," Joké said with a raised brow. "Costume trunk is over there."

Efi nodded, hoping she wasn't showing *too* much enthusiasm.

"Sam!" Joké yelled through cupped hands. "Put that down before something gets broken. We can't afford to damage any more props!"

Efi looked up and saw Sam with the Doomfist gauntlet on, waving it around threateningly at the stagehands. They ignored him. "Hey, Joké, you ever consider turning this play into a rap battle? It might liven history up a bit."

"I'd rather spare the audience from witnessing that particular talent of yours," Joké grumbled. "Now get to work before I reassign you to the part of omnic number four."

Sam grimaced. "You mean the one that gets clobbered by the Talon agents?"

Joké glowered at him.

"Point taken," Sam said, then ran off toward the paint buckets sitting at the bottom of the plywood skyline.

Efi went over to the trunk, started pulling out costumes, and spread them out on the floor. Most seemed in good shape, but a few were a mess, even from their short time of being packed away. Efi activated the ironing wand, and it emitted a warm orange light, but before she waved away a single wrinkle, Naade barged into the theater with Orisa in tow.

"Efi!" he said, completely flustered, arms flailing like a little kid. "Efi, I need your help!"

Efi looked around, embarrassed. Naade was supposed to be training Orisa on fighting tactics during this self-imposed robot hiatus, not embarrassing Efi in front of her new friends. Things had been going so well, but now the students were looking at her again, like she was almost, but not quite, one of them. She excused herself and met Naade halfway down the aisle.

"Naade," Efi said out the side of her mouth. "Can it wait? I'm kind of in the middle of something." Efi spared an awkward glance at her robot, making sure she was doing okay, but she didn't look long. She knew she'd get in trouble if her mother found out she'd gone against her promise of not working with Orisa.

"It can't wait. Something's not right with her," Naade said. "I was teaching her to use her hard-light lasso to grab small objects. You know, so she could do things like pull med packs away from injured people . . ."

"That sounds pretty awful," Efi said with a frown on her face.

"Well, it doesn't matter, because Orisa refused to do it. She said it conflicted with her programming, to protect the vulnerable and to be just and fair. But I told her she didn't understand. I told her that Doomfist didn't care about fair. He wants to cause chaos and wouldn't think twice about hurting anyone who stood in his way. She still didn't get it. So I showed her the . . ." Naade's voice trailed off into a mumble at the end of the sentence.

"You showed her what?" Efi asked.

"The footage from the airport attack."

"Naade!" Efi said. Her heart was suddenly beating hard in her chest as those images came back to her mind. She shook her head. Orisa shouldn't have watched that. She was still too young. Too impressionable. She looked back at Joké. Efi didn't want to let her down, but this was serious.

"Hey, something's come up, but I'll iron those costumes later, I promise," she said to Joké. Joké threw her hands in the air as a fourth person let her down on the ironing, but she quickly turned back to the tasks at hand.

Efi initiated a diagnostic, and while she waited for the results, her attention was drawn back to the stage. A commotion had started as Sam made his way up to the top of the Numbani skyline.

"Hey, look!" Sam said, raising his Doomfist gauntlet up high. Then he started freestyle rapping, badly, about how his fist was going to crush the competition like a recycler crushes soda cans. Joké shook her head.

"Wow, he's really awful," said Efi said to herself. She turned back to Orisa, but instead of seeing the robot's open diagnostic panel, she was met with the frightening sight of Orisa with her hard-light caster drawn.

"Enemy detected. Preparing to engage," Orisa said, then she took off running down the aisle, weapons raised at Sam.

"Orisa, no! That's not—"

Orisa's fired the hard-light projectiles, and a staccato parade of *thumps* filled the theater. Her aim was perfect, knocking Sam in the head. The punch from the weapon wasn't strong enough to cause much more than a bruise, but it was jarring enough for Sam to lose his footing high up at the top of the fabricated Numbani skyline. He fell fifteen feet, colliding hard with the stage floor.

He screamed out in pain. Efi tried so hard not to look, but when she did, she saw his leg, bent like no leg should ever bend. She looked away, back toward Orisa.

"Threat neutralized," Orisa said proudly, looking to Efi for approval.

"Orisa," Efi's voice squeaked. "You've hurt someone. You've hurt my friend."

"Negative, Efi. I have subdued Doomfist. You have taught me that he is our enemy."

"That wasn't Doomfist. You've made a mistake."

I've made a mistake, Efi thought to herself.

The school nurse ran in, followed by two omnic medics. Efi watched in silence as they stabilized Sam's leg, then hauled him off on a gurney levitating steadily up the slope of the center aisle, followed by Joké and the rest of the worried drama students.

Efi was left with Orisa, Dayo, and Naade.

"I'm sorry. I'm sorry. I'm sorry," Naade said as he paced back and forth. "I should never have showed her that video. It messed up her head."

"It's not your fault. It's mine," Efi said. "She's my creation, and Sam is hurt because of me."

"It was a freak accident," Dayo said. "And Joké warned him not to play around."

Efi shook her head. "It doesn't matter. My—my mother was right. This is too big for me. Every time I try to adjust her programming, I just make things worse. I can't trust Orisa around anyone. She's a threat to everyone." A lump welled up in Efi's throat. She should have listened to her auntie and shut the robot down before something bad happened. Well, it was too late for that, but Efi could make sure that Orisa didn't hurt anyone else ever again.

The king's palace was burned, and it added beauty to it. It was a saying her grandfather had told her on more than one occasion. He'd lived through the worst of the Omnic Crisis, doing triage on the front lines. Even as bullets whizzed past him, even as behemoth omnic constructs threatened to trample him, he still somehow managed to find beauty in the world that surrounded him. Entire buildings lay in ruins, smoldering, yet somehow he clung to the silver lining no matter how bad things got. He knew what he was fighting for . . . *For you, dear,* he'd say to Efi.

But I wasn't even born yet, baba nla, Efi would say to him when he told her this.

You do not yet understand how love works, he'd say to her with a compassionate smile. *Once it exists, it has always existed. And it forever and always will.*

Efi thought about what her grandfather had told her. Efi loved her robot. It hadn't even been a whole month since Orisa first came online, but Efi couldn't remember a time when her heart had been so full. She couldn't imagine a time where she wouldn't love her robot, either. And yet, she knew what she had to do.

Back in the workshop, Efi surveyed the damage—everything she'd sacrificed only to bring her to this low. Her prized tool set was gone. Her computers were glitching. Her award money was tied up for the next nine months now, paying off all the debts she owed in the wake of Orisa's well-intended destruction. All that remained besides a few half-assembled Junies was Orisa's docking bay, and the robot herself.

"Orisa," Efi said solemnly as she led her creation to the bay. "I thought I could make a hero to protect Numbani, but maybe that was asking too much."

Orisa's head cocked and her cross-cut eyes went wide. "Your face is leaking again, Efi. Do you require assistance?"

Efi shook her head. "No, Orisa. I'm okay."

She opened the access panel on Orisa's chassis and keyed in the deactivation code. The tiny screen lit up with green lettering:

```
DEACTIVATING OR15 UNIT

Click Yes to Confirm
```

"I am not ready to be deactivated, Efi," Orisa said. "I have made a mistake, but I am fully capable of learning from my mistakes."

"I love you, Orisa. And I'm sorry."

"I'm still learning!" Orisa cried out suddenly. "I'm still–"

Efi pressed YES.

The robot's golden eyes went dull gray. She slumped forward as the whine of her processors and motors powered down. Efi had misspoken when she'd said that her robot would never hurt anyone again, because nothing could possibly hurt worse than this.

DEACTIVATION SEQUENCE
INITIALIZING

. . .

. . .

. . .

DISENGAGING LOCOMOTION PROTOCOLS

. . .

DISCONNECTING SENSORY ALGORITHMS

. . .

TRUNCATING BIOMETRIC ACCESS

. . .

ARCHIVING PERSONALITY MATRIX
efi_was_here_v3-39x.aipm

. . .

DISABLING SELF-RESTART ACCESS

. . .

DE-INTEGRATING INTELLIGENCE MODULES

. . .

DEACTIVATION SEQUENCE COMPLETE

. . .

. . .

. . .

OR15 UNIT OFFLINE

CHAPTER 15

"Okay, I've only seen *Flash Brighton and the Omnic Crusaders: Forty-Four Hours Till Midnight* eleven times so far," Naade said, shoving a handful of popcorn into his mouth, "so I'm sure I'll pick up some new things. Like I still don't understand why Flash abandons the werewolf pups to go looking for his brother's assassin when he could have thrown them into the time machine and taken them with him."

"Whoa, spoiler alert!" Efi said, nudging Naade in the side. "And how have you seen this movie eleven times? It's only been out a week."

"It's so good, Efi. One of Kam Kalu's best movies ever."

"Better than the Darkspire prequels?" asked Hassana.

"*Nothing's* better than the Darkspire prequels," Naade said. "That's not a fair comparison. Like sure, they both have great underwater fight scenes, and I've heard that the moon race sequences use the exact same footage, but when it comes to Flash's ability to control his enemies' minds–"

Efi shoved her fingers into her ears. "Naade! Can we get through the movie without you giving the whole thing away?"

"Fine! Not another word from me. But when Flash and Doc Clamfire start speaking in the ancient mer-language of the lost city of Manta, don't ask me to translate."

Efi smiled and leaned back into her theater seat. These were the kinds of annoyances she could get used to: too much salt in the popcorn, a friend chatting too much during a movie that promised to be at least three times worse than the trailers hinted at.

Efi's watch hummed, and Naade's number came up on the screen. "The seahorse's wife is the killer!" the text said. Efi's eyes went wide. She threw a piece of popcorn at Naade and it hit him right in the forehead.

"I'm joking!" he said. "I'm joking. She couldn't possibly have done it. Not after that scene where she gets captured by Dagger Sect agents and tossed into the particle accelerator."

Efi bit her lip and rolled her eyes. The movie finally started. Okay, the Kam Kalu movies in general really weren't her thing. She found the fight scenes too drawn out and the dialogue too lyrical for her taste. The visuals, on the other hand, were mesmerizing, and it was nice to let her mind wander and get absorbed into the textures of the world.

Then her watch rang again. She glanced at the number—UNKNOWN, and it looked international. She silenced it, then fell back to the movie, throwing popcorn at the screen during the ten-minute interlude where Flash Brighton learns to play the harmonica in a graveyard haunted by the ghost of his college professor. Naade whispered to Efi that it would go on for another twelve minutes, and if she had to use the restroom, now would be a good time. Efi declined, but Naade made a hasty exit, which was expected since he'd slurped down two mega-sized cups of orange soda. While Naade was gone, Efi's watch rang again, same number. Weird. The prefix seemed familiar. Then she remembered that it was the same as that hotel they'd booked in Rio.

She didn't think . . .

It couldn't possibly be . . .

She answered it anyway, right there in the middle of the theater, her voice a whisper under the heavy rumbling of Flash trying to run the ghost down with a bulldozer. "Hello?"

"Efi Oladele?" the voice asked.

"Yes . . ."

"Hey! Lúcio, comin' at you. Had to call to tell you how much I admire your work and activism for your community."

"Naade, come on. This isn't funny," Efi said into her watch. She was getting tired of his pranks. Not even ten minutes ago, he'd sucked the chocolate off one of his Fuddy Duds before offering it to her. She wished she could say that she hadn't taken it, but the theater was super dark, and she wasn't paying attention, and well . . . she'd rather not think of it. And now he was pretending to be Lúcio on the phone?

"What isn't funny?" Naade said, back from the restroom already.

"Gross! Did you even wash your hands?" Hassana asked.

Naade wiped his wet hands across Hassana's arm, and she screamed. The entire audience shushed them. If Naade wasn't playing a prank on her, then . . .

"Lúcio?" she whispered into the watch. "*The* Lúcio?"

"In the flesh."

Efi wasn't sure at what point she'd started screaming, but when the ushers came for her, she went willingly, with Hassana and Naade following after them. She was pretty sure someone had said something about them now being permanently banned from this theater, but Efi was too busy transferring the feed from her watch to her tablet so they all could see. Lúcio was in his studio with concert posters tacked all over the walls at odd angles, a platinum record award serving as coaster for a giant drink filled with about a dozen lime wedges, and statues of his lucky tree frog in all shapes and sizes lining an entire bookshelf.

"Lúcio," Efi said proudly. "These are my friends Hassana and Naade. I wouldn't be anywhere without them."

"Hi, Hassana. Hey, Naade. Any friend of Efi's is a friend of mine. Listen, I've been following your development of Orisa, and I heard about your Unity Day play fundraiser over there in Numbani. I want to support it."

"You want to buy a ticket to the play?" Efi asked. "Because we'll have a front row seat, just for you! As a matter of fact, you can have the whole front row. You can have the whole theater."

"Nah, not a ticket. I was thinking we could boost sales if we move you to a bigger venue. Say, Unity Plaza? I could follow your play with a concert performance, drop some beats on Numbani. Who's in?"

Efi blinked. "Unity Plaza. That's so—"

"Exciting! Amazing! Perfect!" Naade said enthusiastically.

"Yeah, that, too," Efi said as she nodded. "But I was going to say *big*." Putting on a play for eight hundred people was one thing. Unity Plaza served as the stage for Numbani's biggest outdoor festivals. Putting on a play for fifteen thousand people would be something entirely different.

"I'll arrange the details. Don't you worry about that," Lúcio said. "We'll throw some posters up around the city, build some hype. Maybe get your face on some, too."

"I love you, Lúcio!" Hassana shouted, grabbing the tablet, no longer able to contain her cool. "I've got all your albums, a broken buckle off a pair of your old skates, and some of your beard trimmings that I got off Fanzilla Prime!"

"Ha, your friends are funny," Lúcio said to Efi. "I'll have my people contact your people so we can set this up. Okay?"

"Yeah . . ." Efi said, still in a daze. Did she even *have* people? And how had she not fainted already? "That sounds great."

Play it cool, play it cool. Efi felt the excitement surge through her, starting at the tips of her toes, to her knees, turning into a bubbling mess in her stomach, and filling her lungs with enough air to make the shrillest scream the world had likely ever witnessed. She just had to keep it bottled up for a few more moments.

"Lúcio said my name," Naade murmured to himself. "Yeah, I'm never cleaning my ears again."

"There's one last thing," Lúcio said, but instead of finishing his sentence, he started bouncing his shoulders, his locs flipping this way and that, as if he were dancing to an inaudible beat. He turned away from the camera, humming and beatboxing, then started scratching at his turntable. "You feel that beat? Must be some of your creativity and invention rubbing off on me. Make sure you to bring that robot of yours to the concert. Orisa, right?"

"I—I can't," Efi said, a sudden pit in her heart. She couldn't bring Orisa. She was deactivated, and it was better for everyone if she stayed that way. Efi couldn't bring herself to say no to a request from Lúcio, either. "I can't wait for you to meet her," she muttered.

"Glad we're on the same wavelength. We need to show everyone that people like you and me can make a difference in the world. Catch ya next week!"

Finally, Lúcio disconnected, but the joy Efi had felt was replaced by dread. She couldn't bring Orisa back online. Not after what happened with Sam.

"His voice was so . . . so . . ." Naade said, hugging his giant bag of popcorn to his chest.

"He's putting on a concert here! In Numbani!" Hassana squealed. "What am I going to wear?"

"Oh, you have to let me be there when you tell Dayo," Naade said to Efi. "He's going to flip out."

"We're going to raise so much money for those attack

victims," Hassana said. "We'll be able to rebuild the museum, too! And fix the Adawe statue and add some benches, and flower beds, and–"

"I can't do this," Efi said.

Hassana and Naade stopped dancing and stared at Efi. "Can't do what?" Hassana asked. "Lúcio said he'd get everything arranged."

"I can't bring Orisa."

"You have to! That's part of the deal!" Naade said.

"You don't understand. She's not safe, especially not in a huge setting like that. There're too many variables. What if she gets triggered by the Doomfist costume again? Just wearing a fake gauntlet was enough to make her hurt Sam!"

"So then you'll fix her," Naade said. "You always work out the bugs, Efi."

She suddenly recalled her auntie's words. *Bugs are fine when they mean a half-meter-tall robot bumping into a wall. Bugs are not fine when a two-ton robot puts its fist through the grill of a brand-new Steppe Wanderer.*

"We'll help you," Hassana said, nudging her.

"It's not that easy. Turning off Orisa wasn't just booting off a machine. I turned off part of myself when I hit that switch. I don't want to go ever through that again."

Efi walked out of the theater without looking back.

Efi realized she'd been staring at the same calculus problem for ten minutes. She couldn't concentrate, not with Orisa's empty eyes staring down at her as she studied. She knew the robot was offline, but she still had the sinking feeling that she was being watched. For the first time in her life, she felt like she had to get out of her workshop. Now.

She texted her cousin Dayo and asked if he wanted to study at Kọfị Aromo. He agreed, and they met there an hour later, tablets spread out in front of them, and their laptops and graphing calculators, too. There was barely room on the table for the barista to place their drinks when he came. Efi moved her graphing calculator onto the stool next to her to make room for her coffee. Mostly milk, and more sugar than her parents would be okay with, but she felt like she'd earned it after the week she'd had. She looked up at the barista to say thanks, but her tongue caught in her mouth when she saw his face. He looked so familiar.

"Thanks," she finally managed to say, searching her brain for where she must have seen him. He was youngish, so maybe school.

He smiled a tight smile and set Dayo's tea on the table as well.

"I can't believe Ms. Okorie is giving us a test right before the play," Dayo said, taking a sip of his tea, then regretting it. "Oooh, too hot."

"Doesn't she realize how big of an event this is?" Efi asked. "I bet she would have canceled the test if it were Torbjörn coming to town instead. She'd stay up all night so she could get front row tickets to listen to him talk about abstract algebra and real analysis, and the dangers of weaponized artificial intelligence. Yeah, I like being a math and science nerd, too, but come on!"

"I hear you," Dayo said, commiserating. "Efi, don't let it get you all worked up. Hey, what did the pirate say when he looked at his empty shoulder?" Dayo wriggled his brow like it was an excited caterpillar.

"Polygon." Efi mumbled the punch line. "That was bad."

"Okay, how about this? Why should you worry about your math teacher holding up a holographic graphing calculator?"

"Because," Efi said with a grin and an exasperated head shake. "You know she's plotting something. Like we should be doing. This test isn't going to study for itself."

Efi helped Dayo through indefinite integrals, and then Dayo explained inverse trigonometric functions to Efi. They were making good progress together, until Dayo winced slightly.

"You okay?" Efi asked.

"Yeah. I just need to run to the restroom. Be right back. Don't do problem thirty-four b without me!"

Efi nodded, then practiced going over the scratch work from the previous question again. She pulled the graphing calculator close, spinning the holographic image around and studying it from all angles. She was glad she had her cousin to help her out both in and out of the classroom. He'd made the transition into high school so much easier.

"That was fast," Efi said, still fiddling with her graphing calculator when Dayo sat back down. Her unease grew the moment after the words came out of her mouth. She looked up. It was her cousin sitting across the table, but it wasn't Dayo.

Efi stiffened. She hadn't told anyone what she'd seen at the museum. Her family was too disappointed in Bisi already, getting caught up with area boys in high school, then after that taste of power, he'd worked his way into organized crime, where his intellect was highly prized. She didn't see the need to make things worse by telling her family that Bisi had gone on to become a Talon agent.

Now here he sat. All those memories of the time before rushed to the front of her brain. Like when they'd made invisible ink together and had written all over the walls of Bisi's home. Efi always smiled when she had dinner over there, knowing there was still that invisible dog she'd drawn right next to the china hutch. It pleased her that something so crudely drawn secretly existed in the room her auntie went through such lengths to keep posh and pristine.

"Mind if we chat a bit?" Bisi asked. "It's been so nice to see my little cousin all grown up and so smart." He patted her head. If she wasn't mad at him before, she was now.

"Don't touch me," she growled, hard and firm.

"Sorry, sorry," he said, throwing his hands up. "I've been wanting to talk to you since the museum. I was impressed with how you handled yourself."

"You recognized me?"

"Of course I recognized you! You don't spend four hours hunched over a 3-D puzzle of the Horizon Lunar Colony with someone and forget what they look like."

"So you would have let Doomfist kill me?"

Bisi scoffed. "I believed in you the whole time. I was rooting for you."

Efi wasn't buying it. Not for a second. "What do you want? Dayo will be back any second, so you better spit it out quick."

"Oh, we've got some time. My brother will be tied up for a while, guaranteed." Bisi ran his finger over the rim of Dayo's tea cup, and suddenly Efi realized where she'd recognized the barista from. He'd been one of Doomfist's lieutenants at the museum.

"After all you've done to him, you had to poison him, too?" Efi said, slamming her hands down on the table. Her coffee nearly toppled over, but she didn't care. Or maybe she did. It was still hot enough that she could use it as a weapon if it came to that.

"Just a mild stomach irritant. He'll become intimately familiar with the toilet here, but nothing more. You've got skill, Efi. I'm here to extend to you an opportunity to make a real impact in the world. Do you remember when you wanted a tool set and your parents got you that toy one?"

Efi nodded.

"And who saw that you needed something better? Something you could do real work with?"

"You did," she ground out.

"I did, Efi. And here we are again. Only this time, these are the toys." He gestured at her electronics sitting on the table. "And this is what you deserve to be using." Bisi placed on the table a laptop that looked not much different than her own. When he opened it, instead of the fifteen-inch holoscreen she was used to working on, the holoprojection extended in all directions, creating a cockpit dashboard bigger than their table. He swiped the graphing calculator problem onto the laptop, and it lit up, answers and all, showing all the work in three different variations of proof styles.

It pulled her in. She fed it a set of logic exercises that even the most advanced omnics struggled with, and it chewed through them all in a fraction of a second. Then she had it run AI wire-frame simulations, giving it specifications for a three-legged, top-heavy omnic, with a long appendage extending out back, and then sat back to see how long the wire frames took to figure out how to walk. Within four seconds, it was stumbling around. After six, it was walking steadily. And after ten seconds, it was running faster than a bio-enhanced world-class sprinter. Efi's laptop always choked so hard when she attempted these types of simulations, and she usually had time to make herself a sandwich and catch an episode of the *Overwatch* cartoons before it finished processing.

"You like that, huh?" Bisi said. Efi suddenly sat up, realizing that she'd been fussing with the machine for several minutes. "This is only the tip of the iceberg. Join Talon, and you'll have your own workshop. One that will rival the best roboticists' in the world. This is your chance to stop playing with childish things, Efi. To show everyone you aren't a kid anymore."

Efi and Bisi were drawing stares from the other customers. She slammed the laptop shut and shook her head. "I will not join you. I would never disappoint my parents the way you have. How did you know I would be here anyway? Have you been spying on me?" Efi gulped. Had he hacked her computer? What else did he know about her? And if he knew, then *Talon* knew.

Bisi laughed. "I'm starting to get the feeling that you've bought into all the lies the media has made up about our organization."

"Is the terror the people of Numbani have been suffering a lie? Did Doomfist not break out of prison and steal the gauntlet?"

Bisi leaned back and crossed his arms. "Akande escaped his unlawful imprisonment and reclaimed his own property. He's a hero and a visionary who wants nothing but to protect humanity." Her cousin leaned into the table then, and met her eye. "There are two sides to every coin. Overwatch isn't exactly innocent of shedding blood, you know."

"But they fight for justice and equality. What do you fight for?"

"Power," Bisi said. "The power to shape the world into what it needs to be. To make it stronger. Better. Just like that robot you built. Orisa, right? I've never seen anything like it. You're one of us, Efi. You just haven't accepted it yet."

"I'm *nothing* like you," Efi said. "And there's nothing you can say to change my mind."

Bisi smiled. "Do you ever wonder who nominated you for the Adawe grant? Maybe you ought to use that genius brain of yours to think on that." Bisi looked up suddenly, over Efi's shoulder, with a fearful look on his face. Efi turned and saw Dayo stumbling out of the restroom, hand still clenching his stomach. Efi looked back at Bisi, but he was gone. The laptop remained.

"Ugh," Dayo said, taking an oh-so-delicate seat on the chair. He winced as his rear made contact with the seat. "Something I ate today really messed me up. I think I'm going to have to–" He saw the laptop. "What's this?"

"It's nothing," Efi said, but she couldn't stop staring at it. Had Doomfist been the one who nominated her for the Genius Grant? He had the pull, definitely. And at the museum, he had said that he was a fan of hers, but was he *the* fan who'd signed that anonymous message? Efi shuddered at the thought of owing Orisa's creation to the one person she wanted to bring down.

Efi built Orisa, making sure her robot was as resilient as possible. As powerful as possible, and she owed that to the chaos that Doomfist had caused. On that note, Bisi's argument was sound. It was logical, even, and Efi couldn't help but be intrigued by a good logic problem. However, Efi had also given Orisa compassion. That robot of hers was compassionate to a fault. And it wasn't a flaw, Efi now realized, but a feature that separated people like her from people like Bisi and Doomfist.

"It's nothing," she said again, and this time she felt it through her entire self. She helped Dayo pack up his things and left the laptop where it sat.

CHAPTER 16

Efi made her way home, still shaken from her encounter with Bisi. Her workshop had grown stuffy, so she opened the windows despite the gloom that lurked past the sill. High above in the sky, she saw a Sky Postal delivery drone heading her way, carrying a big box. She shuddered at seeing how high up it was flying, wondering how she'd ever gotten the nerve to ride one. But she knew how. She'd done it for love. She loved Orisa. She always had and always would. She finally understood what her grandfather had meant.

The drone didn't bank left or right; it kept coming right toward her building. Then it zeroed in on her, flew through her window, and deposited the box on the floor. She wasn't expecting a delivery, but her name was on it. She pressed her thumb on the pad to accept it, then the drone took off, back through the window.

Weird.

She carefully opened the box, and when she saw the Volskaya

Industries logo on the inside, she knew immediately what it was. There was a note tucked in with the packing material. She read it:

```
Dear Efi,
I saw your holovid wish list and thought this
would help you get Orisa show-ready. Can't wait
to meet you both in person!

    L
```

A wave of excitement washed over Efi. A miniature Tobelstein reactor. Lúcio had gotten her a reactor! But . . .

But . . .

Big but.

She didn't know if she could use it. Would she ever boot up Orisa again? She walked over to the robot, now a cold metal husk.

Doing something to help protect Numbani hadn't worked the way Efi had wanted it to.

But not doing anything felt much worse.

A knock came on her workshop door. Efi turned around and saw her mother. "Efi—"

"I know, Mama, I know. I'm sending it back."

"That's what I've come to talk you about. The Tumblestone Reactor."

"Tobelstein, Mama."

"That's what I said. Now your father and I are wondering if we've given you too much freedom, because you've got a whole Lúcio chatting us up, asking for permission to give you that reactor."

Suddenly, Efi's head was spinning. "You *chatted* with *Lúcio*?" The casual way her mother had said it, it was like she'd chatted with Mrs. Eni about her cats' dander problems.

"Such a nice boy."

"Boy? Mama, that's Lúcio! *The* Lúcio. He's an international celebrity! Sold out every single seat on his world tour! He's one of the biggest freedom fighters of this century!"

"And so? I said that he was a nice boy. He really believes in you. There are people all over this city who believe in you. Maybe we should have believed harder in you as well. It's made us reconsider."

Efi shook her head. "I tried so hard to make the perfect protector for Numbani, but all she did was destroy stuff and hurt people."

"That's not all she did. She taught you about responsibility. And friendship. She got you out and even more invested in our community. Maybe Orisa doesn't have to be perfect. Maybe she doesn't have to keep Numbani perfectly safe. Maybe if you and Orisa can make the world just a little better, that will be enough." There were tears in her mother's eyes.

"Are you crying?" Efi asked her mother.

"It's hard watching you grow up so fast. But I'm proud of you." She still lingered in the doorway. Efi decided she should invite her in.

"Do you want to help?" Efi asked, holding up a box cutter.

Mother laughed and came into the workshop. She took the cutter and slid it along the seam of the box, revealing the reactor.

"Looks complicated," she said.

"It's mostly plug and play. Easy compared to that Junkertown reactor."

"*Junker* reactor?" her mother said with an arched brow.

"Nothing. Here, let's get this thing out of the box."

They worked together, Efi explaining to her mother as they went. After the reactor was installed, they spent the rest of the afternoon restoring Orisa's compassion module. Efi promised herself it was the last time she'd tinker with Orisa's programming. From now on, she'd let her robot grow organically into whatever she was meant to be. And Efi couldn't wait to see who that was.

"Okay, this is it," Efi said as she was ready to boot her robot back up. "Do you want to do the honors?"

"Oh, Efi, I think I will leave that to you. Just remember the guidelines, and . . . stay safe, okay?" Mother looked like she was about to cry again.

"Do you need a hug, Mama?"

"I'd love one," she said, then squeezed Efi tightly. Efi didn't try to wriggle free. She just enjoyed it. "Good luck." Her mother smiled, rubbed Efi's back one last time, and left her daughter to her work.

Efi initiated the boot sequence and brought Orisa back

online. Efi did a little dance, and Orisa reciprocated, shaking all that titanium in a robotic groove.

"I'm glad to have you back," Efi said.

"It's good to be back," said Orisa. "I am at your service."

"How do you feel?"

"Sad," the robot said after a long pause. "I remember I hurt a boy. He was in pain. Why did you disable my compassion module? I didn't get to apologize to him. To make things right."

Efi shook her head. "I'm the one who should be apologizing to you. It was me who didn't want to deal with compassion. I got so focused on getting to Doomfist and keeping everyone else happy, I didn't consider your feelings. I was wrong, and I'm sorry. But I think I have a way to make it up to you. Lúcio's performing a Unity Day concert, and we've got front row seats."

"Please repeat. I believe my auditory sensors are malfunctioning. It sounded like you said that I am going to Lúcio's concert."

"That's what I said." Efi giggled. "And you'll be the star of the show. But we have to review one very important protocol before the concert," Efi said, then she tapped a button on her tablet, brought up the Lúcio playlist, and pressed PLAY. A hypnotic beat filled the room, and the two friends began to dance.

HollaGram

BotBuilder11 is building robots for Lúcio!

FANS **4582**

HOLOVID TRANSCRIPT
Automatically Generated by TranscriptMinderXL version 5.317

SOLD OUT!!!

I can't believe the Lúcio Concert and Unity Play fundraiser event sold out in less than three hours! I hope you got your tickets. This is going to be epic!

COMMENTS (152)

BackwardsSalamander I've only got a couple seconds before they notice I'm online. There are two of them now. They won't let me leave the house. I think they're plotting something. Please call the authorities.

NaadeForPrez @BackwardsSalamander, is this some kind of joke? I don't get it.

BackwardsSalamander This is the human called Backwards Salamander again. Yes, it is a joke. Hahahahahahahahahahaha.

ARTIST4Life Lúcio! Lúcio! Lúcio! I know we've got good seats. Amber is soooo jealous!

Anonymous088503 I'm sure the concert will be a blast

Read more...

CHAPTER 17

he weather couldn't be more perfect. Then again, Efi was
sure that no rain cloud would dare cast its shadow over
Unity Plaza on the day Lúcio was scheduled to perform. In the
quiet of an early morning Saturday, the view of Numbani couldn't
have been more spectacular. The sun glinted off the sleek skyscrapers surrounding them, and past that, Efi could barely make
out the golden glow of the savanna beyond.

"We are very lucky to live here," Orisa said, standing next to
Efi. Efi spooked at the break in silence. She'd nearly been in a
meditative state.

"Yes," said Efi. She now realized this was Orisa's first time taking it all in. Efi could hear the awe in her robot's voice. Sometimes,
when you live in such an amazing place, it just becomes normal,
but seeing it now, through Orisa's eyes, Efi felt re-energized.

From behind them, someone cleared their throat. Efi spun
around and nearly fell over the balcony railing when she saw
who it was.

Lúcio stuck out his hand and grabbed hers, pulling her back to safety. Then he nodded, the large beads at the ends of his locs clacking against each other. "Lúcio Correia dos Santos at your service. You must be Efi," he said, skates moving backward and forward, like he was effortlessly treading water on cement. The skates seemed so much larger in person, big blue and green haunches that ran from his hips to his feet, the hard-light energy buzzing so intensely that Efi could feel it vibrating through the heels of her boots. Efi stood there in shock. She knew she was going to meet Lúcio today, but somehow, she hadn't fully prepared herself with how amazing it would be to stand so close to her biggest hero.

Lúcio smiled as he shook her trembling hand, then his eyes went wide, as if he didn't know whether to be intimidated or impressed by the robot standing next to her. Maybe he was both. "And, whoa, this . . . this is Orisa? Unreal!"

"It's so nice to meet you in person," Efi finally managed to utter. "This is like a dream come true." Efi's thoughts surged through her brain. She didn't know where to start. She wanted to thank him—for this fundraiser concert, for the reactor, for believing in her. Efi knew that as soon as she opened her mouth, senseless blather would fall out, and she had to keep her cool in front of her hero. So instead, she kept it calm and simple. "How has your stay in Numbani been so far?"

Apparently Orisa wasn't as successful at containing her excitement—her rear end wagging like an excited puppy dog, her head cocked and her eyes starry . . . like literally, her eyes had reconfigured into the shape of stars. Efi hadn't even known they could do that.

"This is my kind of city! Everyone's free to live how they choose. Friendly faces, sweet acoustics. And the coffee is kickin'," Lúcio said, raising the to-go Kọfị Aromo cup in his hand. The jet lag was probably getting to him.

"I study at Kọfị Aromo sometimes. I like their tea, too. Sometimes I get hot cocoa. I think it's just Milo, but they put lots of whipped cream on it, so I don't care." Efi gritted her teeth. Was she really making small talk with Lúcio? The only thing worse than geeking out in front of Lúcio was lulling him back to sleep with talk of her favorite hot beverages. "I'm boring you, aren't I?"

Lúcio laughed. "Nah, it's nice to have a normal conversation with someone. Really, Efi, what you did with Orisa, what you're doing with your community, I think it's amazing." He took a turn around Orisa, stopping when he came to the supercharger. "Hey, this is painted up to look like one of those talking drums . . . gangan, right?"

"Yes, but it doesn't work," Efi said.

"Orisa, you mind if I jam with it for a minute? I'm pretty sure superchargers share some tech with my sonic amplifier."

"I would be honored," Orisa said with a bow, then in a single graceful motion, she unmounted her supercharger and placed it on the ground.

Lúcio pulled a set of tools out of his backpack and got to work breaking down the device until he had a pile of components laid out in front of him. "You know, I've been checking out your holovids," he said as he worked. "I've seen all the troubles you've pulled through. And your vision for your city resonates right here." Lúcio tapped his chest with his fist.

"Thank you," she said. "I feel the same about you and what you've done for Rio. And what you've done for the world. How do you have such confidence?"

"I started small, just like you, by making changes in my favela. Did my best to make sure all the kids got healthy meals and all the libraries had books to lend. I surrounded myself with good people who also wanted to make a difference." He winked at Orisa, and she waved back. "I did what I could to make sure my people had healthy bodies and healthy minds, so we could work together to solve our other problems."

"Problems like the Vishkar Corporation?" Efi asked.

Lúcio nodded, then grabbed a set of wires from the pile of components. After inspecting them, he tossed them to the side and crimped off a fresh set from his wire spool. "When my father got mixed up with Vishkar, that's when I really started to see the world for what it was. My father worked as engineer on some of their most lucrative projects. He gave them his best years, his best ideas. Ideas he wanted to share to help the world, but Vishkar turned them to bad ends. They stopped seeing communities and instead saw pawns in a game where they controlled every move and action."

Lúcio smiled, but Efi saw the pain hidden behind it. She'd heard about how Vishkar had treated the citizens of Rio—stark working conditions with low pay, senseless curfews, and questionable laws, all in the name of the so-called greater good. The citizens had revolted and driven Vishkar out of some neighborhoods, but it had taken many rallies and uprisings. And there had been many, many losses.

The message hit Efi even harder when she realized the price she'd paid for Orisa. Orisa had harmed as much as she'd helped. She was learning and growing, but Efi would always be responsible for her robot's actions, whether they be good . . . or not so much.

"That must have been hard, seeing them use your dad's technology like that."

"It was, but you know, my dad designed sonic tech to make the world a better place. When I took it back and used it to rally our people, I was fulfilling the promise my dad had made to them. In the end, I don't think my dad would have regretted what he created."

Efi looked to the horizon, no longer fearful of what was to come. For the first time in a long time, she was hopeful. She'd put so much of herself into Orisa. Time. Money. Her whole heart, practically.

"Wait . . ." Efi said. "Was that reactor you gave me stolen?"

Lúcio shrugged, then shoved the supercharger components back into the case. There were still several parts left over, but he didn't seem concerned. "I've been hanging with a new crowd lately, one looking to do something to help fix our world. I'm honestly not sure where they got it, but I know Katya Volskaya's tech doesn't usually come cheap or easy. And Orisa, if anyone asks—"

"The reactor feels completely paid for to me," the robot said.

"You've got a wicked sense of humor, Orisa," Lúcio said.

"Error 404: Sarcasm module not found," Orisa said flatly.

Lúcio snapped the supercharger's case back together, then set it on one end.

"Thanks for everything you're doing to help," Efi said to Lúcio. "The development has been a little bumpy, but I'm feeling good about things again, like maybe Orisa will one day become the hero Numbani deserves."

Lúcio shook his head. "Numbani already has the hero it needs, and her name is Efi." He gestured at the crowd starting to mill around, staking out the best seats to catch Lúcio's performance in front of the plaza's rhino statue. "Hundreds of thousands of naira have been raised for the victims of Talon's attacks, and that's just from ticket sales. There are more donations coming in by the second. And none of this would be happening if it weren't for you."

Efi was knocked speechless by the idea that she was a hero, but it had to be true. *Lúcio* had said it.

She opened and closed her mouth like a fish.

"What do you say we get this party started a little early?" Lúcio asked.

Efi nodded. "Orisa, would you like to do the honors?"

Orisa activated the supercharger, and the beat pulsed

through them. It was intense, and within seconds, Efi could feel it in her chest, like a new, stronger heartbeat. The heartbeat of a hero.

"Woo, you feel that?" Lúcio started bobbing his head. "Orisa, amp it up!"

Orisa complied and the beat grew louder. Adrenaline flowed through Efi, and she suddenly felt like she could scale the rhino statue in front of them in three seconds flat. She felt like she could punch a hole in the sky. She felt like she could dance forever.

Lúcio's wide shoulders started swaying, and then, all three of them were moving to the beat of the supercharger. He reached behind his back, then with a quick tug and a flash of green light, he released his virtual turntables. Music pumped through his backpack speaker as he scratched beats. Orisa danced, too, shuffling her four legs and pumping her fist in the air.

The dance didn't last forever, but Efi would remember this amazing moment for the rest of her life. Each and every hair on Efi's neck stood on end, and her senses were heightened. She was ready for the concert, for sure.

"Looks like it's good to go," Lúcio said, tossing the super-charger back to Orisa. "We'll talk more after the concert. Hope you like your seats. I picked the menu myself." He gestured at a private balcony, set up with a buffet table lined with treats and a dozen chairs. Yeah, like they'd be sitting down for a single second of the performance.

Then Lúcio took his leave, skating away, leaving Efi's mind

spinning. This was all too perfect! She got out her tablet and texted Hassana and Naade.

> Where are you? I just met Lúcio.
> I DANCED with him.

> We're stuck in security.
> Line is TOO LONG. Crying.

> It's ridic down here. Nobody knows what's going on. Can't figure out where to go.

Efi looked down as the crowd filtered in. They did seem to be understaffed, and with the event scheduled on such short notice, it was understandable.

"Looks like we're on usher duty," Efi said to Orisa. "Let's get people to their spots so everyone has a great time."

"Priority objective: maximum concert fun," Orisa said. And together, they rushed down to the festival grounds. The streets were all blocked off from traffic, creating a makeshift amphitheater, and with the stage perched up on a high balcony, there wouldn't be a bad seat in the house. Efi flashed her VIP pass at the security team, a mix of humans and omnics. One of the omnics scanned it and allowed Naade and Hassana through. Efi handed them their passes.

Naade huffed. "It's about time. I can't believe you met Lúcio without us!"

"Relax, you'll see him after the concert. He can't wait to meet you both."

"Really? He said that?" Naade's feet had practically left the ground from excitement.

"Well, not those exact words, but he did say that any friend of mine is a friend of his."

"So me and Lúcio are BFFs, is what you're saying," Naade agreed. "We go back. Way back. To that call last week, to be exact."

"Where are our seats?" Hassana asked.

"Up there." Efi pointed to the balcony.

Their jaws dropped. "We'll practically be sitting on his amps!" said Hassana, pointing at the collection of speakers, each of them nearly as big as Orisa.

"Say good-bye to my eardrums," Naade said, his grin nearly rabid. "This is the best day of my life."

"There are earplugs up there," Efi said. "And snacks, too. Don't eat them all, Naade."

"Any chance of nose plugs?" Hassana asked. "Naade went heavy on the cologne."

"Well, I'm not meeting Lúcio smelling like my dad's gym bag."

"We're at an outdoor concert. Everyone's going to smell like your dad's gym bag by the end of it."

Naade and Hassana continued bickering, but Efi noticed the crowd starting to swell. "You two go get comfortable. Orisa and I are going to help out down here a bit."

"Yeah, okay," Naade said, tugging Hassana by the elbow. Hassana gave a worried glance back at Efi but went anyway.

Then Orisa got to work. With her compassion module back in place, she was perfectly welcoming to all the fans. She asked if people needed help finding their seats, and if they did, she escorted them and made small talk. Everyone was excited to meet her, and she even signed some autographs and took pictures with people as well. At first, Efi followed nervously behind Orisa as she reunited parents with their lost child and cleared a path through the crowds for people with mobility devices. The robot never missed a beat, bowing and smiling and saying please and thank you. Orisa was the most polite and gracious robot Efi had ever seen. It was like watching her creation grow up, right before her eyes. As the morning progressed, Efi's nervousness faded, and she was confident enough that she could watch her robot from a distance.

Finally, a few minutes before the show started, Efi and Orisa rushed back to their seats. Naade and Hassana were there, filling little plates up with tastes of Afro-Brazilian food. There was akarajé, peeled beans smashed into balls, deep fried, then topped with bits of shrimp—basically the same akara that Efi would stuff in her mouth at festivals. And acaçá, a very special food made of jellied corn flour wrapped up in banana leaves, was the same eko Efi often had with breakfast.

"They've got puff puffs!" Naade said with two of them stuffed in his mouth.

"I think that's pão de queijo," Efi said, though the small round cheese breads did appear similar to puff puff.

"I don't care. Still delicious," said Naade, crumbs tumbling out of his mouth as he spoke.

Efi smiled at her friend, then sighed. Sharing so much culture with Lúcio was definitely bittersweet.

Dayo and Sam and Joké joined them on the balcony. Sam had gotten rapid-X heliotherapy on his broken leg, but he still had to wear the boot for a few more days until everything was completely set.

"There they are! Our heroes of the hour!" Dayo said. Everyone applauded. Instead of being embarrassed for standing out, Efi was proud of what they had accomplished. Dayo pointed up at the stage. A miniature version of the Numbani skyline sat dwarfed by the real thing. They both were absolutely beautiful. "How does the set look?"

"You did an amazing job," Efi said. "I can't wait to see your play. Are you nervous?"

"Not at all. Everything's going to be great. I can't tell you how excited we are to finally get a chance to perform!"

Orisa stepped forward and stood before Sam. "I am sorry for hurting you," she said. "Is there anything I can do to make amends?"

Sam grinned. "I choose to believe that the reason you shot at me was because I was the most convincing Doomfist anyone has ever seen."

"Yes," Orisa said. "Yes, that is exactly it." Apparently, her sarcasm module was working just fine.

"Anyway, we'd better get onstage," Dayo said with a shrug. "We just wanted to say hi! And thanks."

"You'll do great. Break a—" Efi stopped herself. "Have fun up there," she said instead.

The crowd cheered when the actors took their places, chanting "Unity! Unity!" as Joké stepped forward and spoke into the mic.

She pointed to the electronic meter to the right of the stage. "If you like what you see up here, if you're enjoying yourself, please show your appreciation by donating. We're trying to raise two hundred million naira to help the victims of Talon's attacks. Every donation counts. There's no amount too small . . . or too large for that matter!" Joké laughed. "Now, I'm pleased to finally present to you, our Unity Day play."

The play went off without a hitch, the entire audience hanging on to Dayo's words as he read the Declaration of Unity. When he finished, the only dry eyes in the house belonged to omnics, but if they could have cried, they would have. There was no way anyone could watch that and not feel proud of being a part of Numbani. And Orisa didn't even flinch when Sam stepped forward, dressed up in his Doomfist outfit. Finally, the actors took their bows, and the audience cheered. Efi was so proud of her cousin and drama friends.

Then, to Efi's surprise, Tonal Abyss walked onto the stage, her favorite omnic pop band from when she was a kid. The opening act had been kept a secret, and she was glad to see them, even if she'd outgrown their music.

Constantine stepped forward from the group, holding hands with Gaxx Gator, then they raised their locked fists into the air in a unified motion. The crowd roared.

"We have been moved by recent events," Constantine said, "and with so many forces trying to drive us apart, Tonal Abyss decided that we can no longer let divisions within our group keep us from making awesome music."

"So we've settled on a new time measure," said Gaxx Gator. "Quantum clock Numbani, in honor of the young inventor and her friends who've so diligently stood up to the menace trying to divide their city."

Naade grabbed Efi's and Hassana's hands. "Please be talking about us! Please be talking about us!" he chanted.

"Efi Oladele," said both Constantine and Gaxx Gator in unison, "could you and your friends please give us a little wave?" The enormous spotlight swiveled in Efi's direction, completely bathing her vision in a harsh white light. She pulled her friends close, and they all waved in their best guess of the direction of the stage. "This song is dedicated to you. Keep doing what you're doing."

The song started off with a monotone beat, and one by one, each of the thirty-eight omnic voices folded into the song, singing in a harmony that was so intense, it resonated through Efi's bones. The audience loved it as well, and below, she could see thousands of people swiping donations on their tablets. Holographic coins tumbled through the air, rising like bubbles as they made their way toward the fundraiser thermometer. By their third song, the meter was hurtling toward the two-hundred-million-naira mark, and as the final chords played and the voices faded, it blasted right past it. They'd reached their goal already, and Lúcio hadn't even performed yet!

Moments later, a smoke bomb exploded on the stage—blue, purple, and hot-pink laser light erupting from it. Then the beat dropped.

When the fog cleared, Lúcio was standing there at his turntable, and the crowd roared. He started to sway with the music, completely absorbed by the sound. Like it was alive. Efi wondered if Lúcio felt the same way about his music as she did about building and programming bots.

"He's playing 'We Move Together as One'!" Naade shouted after the first two notes of the song.

Efi let her head sway, her body sway. The beat completely took over her mind. Next to her, Orisa was doing the same, and Naade and Hassana, too, and beyond that, the whole entire audience was caught up in the hypnotic rhythm.

Here Efi was in her favorite city, surrounded by her favorite friends including her favorite robot, watching her favorite artist perform her favorite song . . . and in just a few seconds, Lúcio would get to her favorite part of the song, right where the tempo switched up on you—that part that made your toes curl up and your skin go to goose flesh and your body become a rag doll.

This . . .

Part . . .

Right . . .

But instead, a high-pitched whine whistled from above the

stage, followed by a column of blue light. The crowd cheered below, thinking it was another pyrotechnic display. The music kept going, but Efi could tell something was wrong. Lúcio looked all around, suddenly on high alert, and then his eyes locked with Efi's. The light spread, forming a concentric pool at Lúcio's feet. He leaped out of the way as the thunder of a deep laugh competed against the boom of the bass.

And though Efi couldn't see where it was coming from, she knew who it belonged to. It was a voice she could never forget.

Doomfist.

The skies crackled, and the hairs on Efi's arms rose.

"Orisa!" Efi screamed, but the robot was already on it.

"Enemy detected. Establishing defense point," she said, slinging out a shield in front of the crowd below as a blur descended from nowhere, the a streak of blue lightning catching Efi's attention right before the entire stage was pounded. Orange electrical flames shot up from cracks breaking through the concrete. Chunks of rocky debris and metal shrapnel hit Orisa's barrier, but it held firmly.

When the smoke cleared, Doomfist was standing onstage, his massive arms outstretched, bidding the crowd to cheer for his epic entrance. The deep brown of his skin was painted over in white markings that honored the spirits. He had written his intentions of victory upon his skin as well, declaring that he was already the winner in a battle that had not yet begun. The panicked audience scrambled to get away from him, but they were crammed in too tightly, and escape was impossible.

CHAPTER 18

"**N**ow where is my hero's welcome?" Doomfist yelled into the crowd.

"You are not a hero!" Efi called out. "And you are *not* welcome here!"

Doomfist's eyes cut toward Efi. "You test my patience," he said, then blasted Orisa's barrier several times with his hand cannon. Efi fought everything within herself not to flinch.

Lúcio snuck up behind Doomfist and shot him with his sonic amplifier. A flurry of sound pulses slammed into Doomfist's back and he went flying off the edge of the stage. Doomfist looked back and gave Lúcio a dirty grin before raising his gauntlet. As he fell, the people below pushed and shoved, crawling all over one another to get out of his way. Right as Doomfist landed, he slammed the ground with his gauntlet, sending out a seismic disturbance. The Earth trembled, and the screams intensified. Several of Doomfist's lieutenants descended from the surrounding buildings, like sleeping gargoyles waking up, ready for battle.

"We've got to get the people to safety," Lúcio shouted up to the balcony. "Orisa, I can protect them with my sound barrier if you can distract Doomfist."

"Affirmative. Executing pre-combat routines. Optimizing strategy," said Orisa, leaping down onto the stage beside him.

"The audience will be protected from Doomfist, but what about the Talon soldiers?" Hassana asked. "Can Orisa take them? She hasn't really had any combat training yet, has she?"

"I've got you covered," Lúcio said as he jumped over the railing, skates leaving trails of green light as he rode down the wall like he'd forgotten how gravity was supposed to work. He pushed his way toward the most vulnerable part of the crowd, those nearest to Doomfist. "Oh, let's break it down!" he shouted as he activated his sound barrier, providing the audience with protection as they fled to safety. Then he aimed his sonic amplifier at nearby Talon agents and started firing.

Orisa galloped toward Doomfist like she was ready to seek revenge. Efi leaped down from the balcony and then the stage, knowing that between Lúcio's barriers and Orisa's defenses, she would be safe.

She hoped.

In any case, she helped to herd people toward the exits, doing her best to calm their fears. Hassana, Naade, and the drama club worked on the outer sections of the crowd to avoid attracting attention.

"Doomfist, you will be brought to justice," Orisa said, aiming her arm at him.

Doomfist laughed. "My friend, you do not want to get in the way of this. Go and sit down, and I will allow you and your friends to live."

"He's stalling for time," Efi shouted. "Attack him."

But it was too late. Doomfist's gauntlet had already recharged. He punched it into Orisa's barrier. It lit up brilliantly from the impact, but held tight. They circled each other, Doomfist attacking, Orisa defending. With all of Orisa's upgrades, she was finally an even match for him, and with Lúcio's help, there was no way they could lose.

A series of blasts from nearby Talon agents hit right near Efi's feet, so she scrambled back to the wall and hid behind an enormous speaker, out of harm's way.

"Do not let this robot live," Doomfist commanded his lieutenants. They trickled in from behind Orisa, pelting her with bullets. She turned and redeployed her shield, but it left her exposed to Doomfist. He shot her with his hand cannons, bullets nicking her metal as he recharged for another big attack.

Lúcio jumped up, aimed his sonic amplifier near Orisa, and drove it into the ground. She shuddered when the sound wave hit her, and then a faint green glow engulfed her—providing her with her own personal barrier.

Lúcio distracted the lieutenants, engaging his crossfade while skating circles around them. Then he started taking them out one by one with his sound waves. He was moving so fast, Efi could barely keep her eyes on him as the music coming from his backpack speaker filled Unity Plaza with an energizing beat. Efi glanced back at Orisa, but she wasn't fighting. She was standing there dancing as Talon agents attempted relentlessly to shoot through the green, undulating barrier surrounding her.

"What are you doing, Orisa?" Efi shouted.

"Efi Protocol #4: When Lúcio drops a beat, stop whatever you're doing and dance."

"Override that protocol," Efi said. "Help Lúcio!"

Immediately, Orisa took on a wide-legged stance, fists raised and ready to fight.

Efi felt helpless as she watched from behind the speaker, but she did notice how well Lúcio and Orisa worked together, the beat from his crossfade helping them to coordinate their attacks. Orisa's supercharger had done something similar, right after Lúcio had fixed it.

"Orisa, throw out your supercharger!" Efi called.

Orisa slung the supercharger out. It landed hard on its end, filling the entire plaza with a unifying beat. Orisa and Lúcio moved in sync and covered for each other as they took the Talon agents out.

But someone else must have noticed how the supercharger was making them work together, because one of the lieutenants escaped the fighting and ran toward it. It was Efi's cousin. He raised his gun, aimed it at the supercharger, ready to destroy yet one more thing.

"Bisi," Efi yelled at her cousin. "Don't do it."

He smiled. "Little cousin. I gave you the chance to be on the winning side. You chose not to take it."

"Well, now I'm giving *you* a chance. The chance to be on the right side. It's not too late. I miss my cousin. I miss the person you used to be."

Bisi shrugged, then blew the supercharger into bits, pieces of electronic equipment scattering all over the place. The beat faded. All that was left were the sounds of terror. "Compassion is a weakness," he said. "Doomfist taught me that."

Without the supercharger, Orisa and Lúcio fell out of sync and lost their tactical advantage.

"Look what you've done!" Efi screamed at him. Bisi only smirked and ran back to rejoin the fight. He distracted Lúcio long enough for Doomfist to catch him with an uppercut to the chin.

Lúcio went sailing into the air, his sonic amplifier flying out of his hand with such a force that the cable snapped. It hit the ground twenty meters away from him with a horrid *crack*. It took Lúcio a moment to shake off the hit, but by the time he did, three lieutenants stood between him and the amplifier. He slowly got to his feet, raised his arms up in defense, then, using the balance and momentum of his own body, swung his leg high into the air, the heel of his skate catching the chin of one of the lieutenants. Efi was impressed with Lúcio's capoeira, the same dance-fighting that her people practiced. The lieutenant wasn't as moved by the display and raised his gun, firing at Lúcio.

Lúcio started skating, as fast as he could, but he couldn't outrun their bullets forever.

It wasn't looking good out there. She had to do something. Efi looked at the sonic amplifier sitting out in the open, the Brazilian tree frog symbol on the front staring at her, like it was waiting for her to do something. What could she do? She didn't know how to fight. Efi had asked her aunt Yewande to teach her capoeira once. She'd seen the old holopics from when her aunt had practiced the martial art as a teen, but that was before the Omnic Crisis, and Aunt Yewande didn't talk about things before the Crisis.

And now a new crisis was unfolding, right here, and Efi felt powerless to stop it.

"I thought you were supposed to bring luck," she yelled at the frog.

Still, the frog stared back at her.

And slowly, Efi's mind started to churn, and she couldn't keep from wondering how Lúcio's sonic amplifier worked. Efi realized that while she couldn't fight with her body, she could fight with her brain. She gathered her courage, and stealthily snuck down to retrieve the device amid the chaos of flying rubble. She studied the insides, then glanced back at the mess left of the concert's massive sound system. If she could reconfigure the pieces and make a giant sonic amplifier, it might give them a chance of beating Doomfist for good.

"I know that look," Dayo said, sneaking up beside her. "If you've got something planned, I'm here to help."

"Us too," Joké said. "We feel useless out here. We want to fight, too."

Efi looked at Dayo and Joké and Sam, and a few of the other drama students. She'd seen them work together to build amazing things. And she knew they could help her now. She quickly drew up the schematics and assigned everyone a role. Dayo dodged bullets as he retrieved a long stretch of wiring from across the stage. Joké sprinted back and forth, gathering up busted pieces of speakers, as much as her arms could carry. And Sam helped Efi assemble everything, handing her the exact item she needed as she called for them. Efi worked as fast as she could. She couldn't even spare a glance to check on how the battle was going, but it wasn't sounding good. Minutes later, they had a sonic amplifier five meters high and nearly as wide.

Naade went around shoving earplugs into everyone's ears, as below, Orisa and Lúcio were completely surrounded and out of options. Doomfist lit Orisa up with another rocket punch, stunning her. Without her shields, Orisa had no protection. And without his sound barrier, Lúcio was left completely vulnerable as well. Doomfist saw his opportunity to strike. He kneeled for a couple seconds, channeling an enormous amount of potential energy, then jumped high into the air, yelling "Meteor strike!"– gauntlet aimed right at Lúcio.

Efi didn't wait another second before she turned on the sonic cannon. There was no time for testing. No time for bugs. This had to work. She played a single note.

It was so loud, it knocked her off her feet. The glass of the building across the way shattered, and Doomfist was knocked off target, landing several meters away from Lúcio. It was still enough to daze Lúcio, but he pulled himself up and got away. Efi fired again, and the next building over shuddered, a giant crack winding all the way to the top. A gazelle head sculpture was perched at the apex, and all eyes focused toward it as it came barreling down the slope of the building. Doomfist's lieutenants started fleeing, but the head slid toward them, charging like an angry beast. It collided with them and they were knocked back from the impact.

In the confusion, Lúcio was able to regroup, positioning himself behind Orisa as she finally came back online. He crossed his arms and cocked his head to one side. "Why are you so angry?" Lúcio said to Doomfist in a playful tone.

There was a flicker in Doomfist's eyes, just for an instant, but Efi noticed it. A hesitation. A hint of doubt. Doomfist projected a calm and controlling demeanor, but despite the declaration of victory painted on his skin, the outcome of this fight was not yet determined.

"Give up now!" Efi screamed down at Doomfist. "Or we'll play a song that's guaranteed to make you move."

Now Efi and her friends had the upper hand. Bisi and Doomfist backed away from them, toward the edge of the catwalk that overlooked the city, a thirty-meter drop onto one of the busiest streets in Numbani.

"There's nowhere to go now," Lúcio said. "Surrender. I'll bet they even kept your prison cell open for you."

"I'm not going back," Doomfist said.

"Come on, Bisi," Dayo said. "It's not too late to ditch Talon. If you continue down this path, you will only cause more pain for everyone."

Efi swore she saw Bisi's lip tremble. Doomfist must have noticed, too, because the fingers on his gauntlet twitched, and then he struck out and pulled Bisi into the massive fist. Bisi struggled and fought to free himself.

"Rethinking your life decisions?" Doomfist asked Bisi, his voice light, but his stare intense.

"No, Doomfist," Bisi cried out as he was lifted off the ground. His feet kicked back and forth, trying to find the ground . . . "I am still dedicated to the cause!"

"Put him down," Efi demanded.

Doomfist pursed his lips, then moved Bisi over the sheer drop. Now her cousin was struggling to hold on tight. "Take another step forward and he's roadkill."

"Should I fire upon Doomfist?" Orisa asked Efi.

Efi stood there, struck still by terror, seeing her cousin dangling like that. If Orisa fired on Doomfist, he'd drop Bisi. If she did nothing, Doomfist would toss him anyway. There was no answer to give. What would Efi tell her parents? Her auntie?

"Doomfist," Bisi said, his voice cracking at the edges. "I've stood by your side, haven't I? I've done everything I could in my power to serve you well!"

Doomfist laughed. "If you've been by my side, learning from me all this time, then you would know that this is the best way you can serve me now." Then he tossed Bisi over the railing.

"Orisa! Do something!" Efi screamed, pure fear carrying her feet forward toward the railing. Orisa leaped into action. Efi knew the logical thing for Orisa to do was to take out Doomfist and restore peace to Numbani, but she hoped upon hope that her robot would think with her heart.

Orisa hustled faster than Efi had ever seen her move, and the robot fired a green orb over the side of the catwalk. By the time Efi made it to the edge, Bisi was caught by the graviton surge from the Tobelstein reactor and yanked back onto the catwalk. He looked up at Efi, met her gaze, then looked away. Ashamed.

"Doomfist is getting away!" Lúcio said, skating after him, but without his sonic amplifier, he was left with no way of fighting against their enemy. Efi looked up, saw Doomfist look back at her and then jump onto another platform. Then another. He disappeared into the shadows between buildings. Orisa moved to charge after Doomfist, but Efi held her hand up, stopping her.

"It's no use. He's gone," Efi said, her head hanging. "We failed."

"He got away, but we didn't fail," Lúcio reassured her. "The way you worked back there, that was amazing. Your quick thinking saved my life, and the lives of thousands of people. But we'll find Doomfist. And he'll pay."

Efi nodded, but she still wasn't convinced. "I guess, but how can you be so sure?"

Lúcio reached down into one of the crevices in his skates and pulled out a piece of folded paper. He opened it and showed it to Efi. It was a photograph, old tech, not a single holographic overlay. It showed a collection of colorful homes, crowded together and crawling up the side of a steep hill. "I recognize that. That's your old favela," Efi said, very sure of herself.

Lúcio shook his head. "Not my old favela. It's still my home." He pointed to a light blue house no bigger than the nail on his pinkie finger. "Here. That's where I live. And these are my neighbors. The kids who grew up with not much more than a fútbol and an empty lot, having the time of their lives. The musicians jamming on the streets, some of them performing on the same corner since I was a kid. The Yoruba aunties selling akarajé and acaçá at the market." Lúcio winked at Efi, a wink that made the whole wide ocean between their continents all but disappear. "They are who I fight for. I will do everything in my power to protect my favela. That is why I'm sure that we will find Doomfist and bring him to justice."

"But I've seen your home! The white stone condo in Ipanema—the whole eighth floor to yourself, facing the beach and where you skate down the pretty cobblestone roads. 590 Avenida Vieira—" Efi stopped herself, not wanting to sound like she was completely obsessed with him or anything. "You know, the one that was featured on *Cribs 411*."

"That's my studio, and to be fair, I do spend quite a bit of time there," Lúcio admitted. "But I'm back in my favela as much as I can be. Ipanema is nice, but you can't get good pão de queijo there. Not like my vo makes them."

His grandmother, Efi knew from the little bit of Portuguese she'd picked up. She smiled, imagining how deeply Lúcio's roots ran in his neighborhood and in Rio. Numbani was a young city in comparison, but Efi looked out over Unity Plaza and the buildings beyond—where her family lived, and her friends, too. Where Mr. Bankolé had his grocery store. Where Ms. Okorie taught calculus. Efi knew that this was where her roots were tied, and she would protect this city . . . even if it meant battling Doomfist and Talon a hundred times over.

"I meant what I said. You're a hero, Efi. And so is Orisa," Lúcio continued. He took a deep breath, then looked around the plaza as the authorities finally arrived, dressed heavily in armor, but the threats had already been neutralized. They started arresting the fallen Talon agents, including Bisi. Efi cringed as she watched Dayo turn his own brother in. She couldn't imagine how awful Dayo felt but hoped that both the brothers found some closure.

"This world needs heroes like you. Can I count on you to help me out from time to time?" Lúcio said, his voice lowered.

Efi smiled, and though the path ahead of her was unknown and intimidating, a new resolve filled her voice. She would fight for Numbani, and for the world, with every scrap of strength she had. "I will help however I can."

HollaGram

HOLOVID TRANSCRIPT
Automatically Generated by TranscriptMinderXL version 5.410

TEAMING UP FOR SOMETHING SPECIAL

Things are starting to calm down now, and Numbani is recovering from the chaos, but it's been difficult to sleep knowing that Doomfist is still out there somewhere.

All of the faded omnics were cured of their sickness, thanks to the help of the Adawe Foundation. They even found our missing omnic teacher safe and sound, down by the recycling plant. And it seems like some of Doomfist's hacks affected a few of my early Junies, before I started using tighter encryptions. If you were affected, sorry! I've done a hard firmware push and any issues should be resolved.

So all is safe in Numbani for now, and Orisa is continuing to learn and grow as she explores the world. And so am I.

We've got so many adventures on the horizon, and I can't wait to see them unfold.

CHAPTER 19

Efi sat in class, attention fully focused on her calculus teacher. She even had her tablet set to "Do Not Disturb" so she wouldn't be tempted to reach out to her friends. They'd have to wait to talk to her until after school was out. Efi had realized that she could do it all: be a great student, a great friend, a great inventor . . . but she couldn't do it all at once.

So while she was at school, she concentrated on school. And back in her workshop, she'd built a couple of robots to help her fill all the orders for the Junies. From time to time, she'd have to spend her evenings there, but for the most part, her workshop didn't cut so much into her time hanging with Naade and Hassana. It wasn't perfect, but it worked.

"Efi," Ms. Okorie said. "Would you like to solve the problem?"

"Yes, ma," Efi said, and walked up to the front of the class. She couldn't shake the strange feeling on the nape of her neck. She looked back, and the entire class was staring intently at her, their starry eyes watching like they expected her to pull a robot out of her sleeve at any moment.

"I'm just a normal kid," Efi said. A normal kid genius with a flourishing robotics workshop, a refurbished OR15 for a best friend, and superstar Lúcio Correia dos Santos on her speed dial. "You don't have to stare so hard. Or clap whenever I walk into the room. Please?"

A knock came at the door. Before Ms. Okorie could respond, the doorknob twitched, then broke off. Then the door itself flew off its hinges and landed with a loud clatter in front of the classroom. The students all bit back their screams.

"Apologies," Orisa said, wedging her frame through the too-narrow doorway, then, when she was inside, giving the class a little wave with her fingertips. "Efi," she said, now serious. "You haven't responded to my alert."

Efi grimaced at the mess her robot had made and tried not to think about how many months of her allowance it would take to repair it. "Sorry, my tablet notifications are off. Can it wait twenty minutes?"

"I'm afraid not," she whispered to Efi. "There are people in trouble, and they need our help."

Efi suddenly felt the weight of being a hero on her shoulders. It was a weight she was more than ready to bear. Orisa, on the other hand . . . "Are you sure you're up for this?" Efi asked.

"All systems functional. Fusion driver upgrade installed and tested. Current combat simulations indicate high probability of victory."

"Fusion driver?" Efi said, noticing that Orisa's hard-light caster had been replaced with a bulky weapon that definitely looked like it could toss out more than wet, balled-up socks. "Where'd you—"

"We must hurry. She is awaiting our arrival."

"She? Who's she?"

Orisa looked around at the students. Every single eye was focused on her. "I can't say right now. But with luck, our trip will be a short one. A quick sojourn abroad, and then right back to Numbani so your studies aren't interrupted. I will explain further once we are airborne."

"Airborne?" Efi said, jumping to her feet. "Does that mean I finally get to fly on a plane?"

"Affirmative."

Efi smiled. "Then let's do this."

ACKNOWLEDGMENTS

Many thanks to Bola and her family for sharing their lives and memories and Yoruba proverbs with me; to the Overwatch team at Activision/Blizzard for entrusting me with these wonderful characters and helping me to shape their story; to Ehigbor for bridging the gap between Nigerian culture and Overwatch Lore; and to David for the groan-inducing math jokes.

Thanks to Chloe, Lori, and Beth for whipping this manuscript into shape and laughing all along the way.

And to all the Overwatch fans out there, thanks for allowing me to be a part of your community. I hope that this story has made it richer.

NICKY DRAYDEN

is a systems analyst who dabbles in prose when she's not buried in code. She resides in Austin, Texas, where being weird is highly encouraged, if not required. Her award-winning novel *The Prey of Gods* is set in a futuristic South Africa brimming with demigods, robots, and hallucinogenic hijinks. See more of her work at nickydrayden.com or catch her on twitter @nickydrayden.